A WYATT
BOOK for

W

— ST. —
MARTIN'S
PRESS

CALVIN BAKER

Naming the New World

🌿

A NOVEL

A Wyatt Book for St. Martin's Press

New York

〜

FOR MY GRANDPARENTS,

THEIR MEMORIES; THEIR BOOK

Design by Pei Loi Koay

Grateful acknowledgment is given for permission to reprint
the stanza from *Canto General* by Pablo Neruda, translated
and edited by Jack Schmitt. Copyright © 1991 Fundacion
Pablo Neruda, Regents of the University of California.

Library of Congress Cataloging-in-Publication Data

Baker, Calvin.
    Naming the new world : a novel / Calvin
Baker.—1st ed.
      p.   cm.
    "A Wyatt book for St. Martin's Press."
    ISBN 0-312-15178-0
    I.   Title.
  PS3552.A3997N35   1996
  813'.54—dc20
                                        96-29347
                                             CIP

First Edition: February 1997

10   9   8   7   6   5   4   3   2   1

Acknowledgments

Many thanks are due to Fred D'Aguiar and Caryl Phillips, who taught me as much about life as they did about writing; Ian, Billy, Kevin, Leslie, Russell, Rick, Ed, Jeremy, Amy, and Natasha, for their unflagging support; Emily, for believing from the beginning; my agents, Claudia Menza and Richard Derus, for their integrity and understanding; and, finally, to you, Mom, for all the obvious reasons and some that are less so.

And your

blood fell here

In the middle of the country it was spilt,

in front of the palace, in the middle of the street,

so that everyone would see it

and no one could expunge it,

and its red stains remained.

—PABLO NERUDA, *CANTO GENERAL*

My great-grandmother was a witch. She prepared a potion which made my grandfather remember his lives before this one. In his last life he was a gambler, before that a whore, a thief, a queen, and a poet. This is all he remembered, except that when he was still very young his mother gave him a seed which she had brought from the far side of the desert. "This is magic," she told him. "When I die, plant it. It will grow."

My father was a sailor, who sailed all around the world, but my grandfather never left home. His job was to look after his mother's tree. He planted it. It grew.

When I was ten years old I was sent to live with him to learn the uses of magic. He taught me where a child lives before it becomes a child and where a soul goes after it dies, but he could not teach me my own name.

After learning what my grandfather could teach

me, I went out into the world in the way of my parents to find the source of my great-grandmother's seed and to learn the name written in my heart.

With a child's naïveté, on a morning with troubled sky, I left my grandfather's house. "The course back is a long walk through the deserts," he said. "It is the way of our people. The only way." Before I arrived I would collect a special gum that grows on the branch of a certain tree which catches the light under the moon. This tree was twin to the one planted by my great-grandmother.

I would wear a cape of black cow skin. And although I did not know what this costume was for, my grandfather told me that my father wore the same garment when he left home. I would eat my hunger on the way. "These are the ways of the desert and the rituals of our people."

On the morning that I left, I awoke to find my father standing over me. "You know that this is foolish," he said.

"Yes, sir."

"And that you are returning to nowhere."

"Yes, sir."

"That there is no past for us."

"Yes, sir."

"And no beautiful tomorrow."

"But . . ."

"Death."

"Yes, sir."

"You will not last."

"Thank you, sir. I understand and place myself at your feet."

My father was a failure. He has spent most of his life ravaged by memory. I left the house and went into the world to die. I did not want to be like my father.

Ampofo

Without a word, he pushed me through the door of the hut, then turned and left. I immediately felt the smallness of the room pressing against my senses. The absence of light and the smell of cooking mixed with the sweat of bodies beat against me as the door fell closed, and misery circled me like memories of the ship's hold.

I stood there in the doorway as my eyes adjusted to the darkness and waited for his footsteps to fade away. When I thought that he had moved far enough into the distance, I shoved anxiously at the door. To my surprise it gave easily. I stepped back outside and peered around the edges of the building. A few children passed me and waved, then continued on without a second glance. I peered again into the darkness of the musty room. In the back I could make out the image of furnishings. As I re-entered the hut, my mind raced to figure out what was happening. I knew that I was a prisoner, but the door to my cell had flown miraculously open. Something was dreadfully wrong.

The sound of a woman's voice startled me. I turned in the direction that the voice had come from and was overwhelmed by her smell. A musky perspiration mingled with spices and a wet floweriness. She smelled robust and delicate as a newborn, but more than anything, she smelled like a woman. This scent competed with the other images for space in my mind, fighting to overpower everything else.

I turned my head away and back toward the door. As she approached me she began speaking in the same ugly tongue as the white men. I did not understand, but I responded to her in the only word I knew in that language.

The sound of her laughter made my ears hot with shame, then fear. But she continued to move closer as I pushed against the wall, making my body as small as possible. She walked with the sway and swagger of complete confidence and, when she finally crossed the short distance between us, touched my face with familiarity. I turned my eyes toward the dirt floor.

Putting her finger under my chin, she pulled my head back up and touched her lips to mine. Her fingers felt firm and tender on my face. It was the first kind touch that I had received since they took me from my home, and my fear began to lift. But as I felt my heart beating again, its sound frightened me.

When I finally accepted the fact that she meant me no harm but only kindness, I thought that perhaps I was being rewarded for some good deed done on my journey. I flashed over the trip through the water and then the short journey over the land, looking for something exceptional that I had done

4

or that the others had not. The only thing I could think of was surviving.

She touched my face again and the blood inside me began to loosen and run hot, the weight of this feeling made me want to cry. It was too kind. They had been too cruel. I could not trust this. Sensing my anxiety, she touched a hand to her chest and said, "Sally."

I touched my own chest and replied, "Sal-ly." She laughed again and I winced. I wanted so badly to make her happy but nothing I did seemed right, that is why the people of the village had sold me, because I soured everything I touched.

She pointed to her chest again and I did the same. Finally I figured out that she was trying to tell me her name, "Sal-ly." I laughed at my foolishness. She must want to know mine. I looked into her eyes, which felt soft as they moved over my body. I told her, not the name that the whiteman called me but the name of my father's house. As soon as I said this though I began to feel nauseous. It did not belong here. It was as distant as a day-old dream. I thought of my father tending his cows and began to think that maybe my home and life before the journey had simply been imagined. But when she repeated the name it sounded beautiful on her tongue. Her accent made it sound alive.

She took hold of my hand and began to trace the lines of it. "Ampofo," she said. Then she pulled me toward the bed and made a space for me beside her. The pressure in my head was dizzying, threatening to tumble me as I made my way over. When I touched her face a charge went through my hands and I began to laugh from the pleasure of it. She began to laugh also as we fell backward holding one upon the other.

For the first time I began to forget about the last six months. The ship, the waters, the smells, all faded to the back of my mind. I wanted only to be here with this woman called Sally, who spoke in their ugly tongue but who looked like she had come through the waters too.

I pulled her closer and began to speak to her in my own language, but had no way of making her understand. "Just hold me," I thought as I stroked the curves of her body and pressed my hand into the small of her back. "Just hold me," as I traced the line of her thighs with my tongue, tasting the saltiness of her flesh. The soft mound of her breasts rose and fell beneath me and the cool sweat of her neck and chin mingled with mine as I laughed uncontrollably. Finally, I kissed her deep eyes and she carved my back with her nails.

When we came we panted and sobbed and cried. But mostly there was laughter as I began to think that this place would be bearable. And I stayed inside of her, blowing softly on her belly to cool the moisture that clung there.

After the laughter died away, I rolled onto my side next to her. She stretched her body, leaving one hand on my hip. Avoiding my eyes, she reached her other hand behind the bed and pulled out a small knife fashioned of steel.

Sally

Master brought in the biggest, blackest man I have ever seen. This one was probably right off the boat, and hadn't stopped to wash that closed-space smell from his body.

As soon as Master left, he pushed at the door looking for an escape. The door was unlocked. He went outside, then came back. The fool did not know that there was no way out. "Do you want it locked?" I asked. He jumped like a frightened animal. As I rose from the bed, I could smell the sweat of the last man still locked in my sheets. I wondered if this one was the kind that liked the smell of another man's sweat.

He stayed cowered in the doorway though, not knowing what to do. I walked over and he dropped his head. "Ain't nothing down on the floor to see," I told him. Then I asked him his name as I pulled his face up to meet mine.

"Nigger," he said.

At first I laughed out loud. Then I realized that this was the only thing he knew and I wanted to hold him, wanted to protect him from the pain that he didn't even know about yet. He just stood there, unable to look into my eyes. Like a child who had done something wrong, he hung his head.

He couldn't hide though. Couldn't hide that he wanted me, was lonely for someone and it did not matter who. It did not matter what would happen later either. He did not know that we were just dogs, being mixed and matched.

I held my hand to my chest and told him my name. Like the parrot in Ramsey's study, he mocked my gesture and words. I began to laugh at him but the hurt in his face made me stop. "Sal-ly"—that's all he said. The rest I just knew. He didn't have to say anything. Looking on his broken-down eyes and that body straining against itself, I wanted to kiss him. I wanted to cry. He looked so confused.

This was the first time that Ramsey had brought somebody in right off the boat. I had seen them all though. White men who came in here whispering all kinds of lies. As if whispering something made it true. Then the black men who came in here almost ashamed because they knew that they were just making more slaves for Ramsey, but their shame never stopped them from doing what they came for. None of them ever looked at my face. They just jumped on top of me and went about their business.

I didn't ever have to coax them and this one certainly did not look like he was a stranger to a woman's bed. I stroked his face. I could see why Ramsey had brought him over to me so fast. His rough hands and powerful back looked as if work was bred in his bones. I held my hand to my chest again and repeated my name. Finally he figured out that I wanted to know his.

"Ampofo."

When I repeated the name it tasted like fresh air to me. He still had his own name. In a year he will have forgotten that he was ever called anything other than the name that Ramsey gave him. He didn't know what he was getting into, but for now his name was still Ampofo. I pulled his face up until our lips met. The cool taste of spit made me feel good. Our mouths fit together so easily, every open space filled by lips and smooth tongue.

I led him toward the bed and he began to laugh like a maniac, circling his arms around me as we fell backward.

I had spent my entire life making babies for Ramsey. Each of them had been born with strong arms and a loud wail, but the important thing was that they were born alive. They breathed their first breaths and were snatched away into the world as painfully as they had come into it. I never knew if the next man to walk through my cabin door would be my own son. I didn't want to bring any more babies into this world. I tried to steel my mind against his touch until there was nothing left in me. No love, no hate, and no memories. I tried to lock them all inside my heart and let scar tissue form around them. I am all scar tissue.

But when he touched me my mind began to give itself to the pleasure. I struggled not to forget that it was only a moment of pleasure.

That's what he didn't know, that it was just a moment that would be snatched away as easily as it had been given. But the ease of his fingers on my body and the tightness of his skin against the muscle made me give in. So many men that I had lost count and his touch made me feel new again.

We laughed with the freedom of that moment and I gave myself to him, really gave in to those fingers and that tongue. But nothing could make the thoughts of this place cease. His hands, as tender as they were, were still the touch of one of Ramsey's slaves. His smile would always be to keep Ramsey's whip away from his flesh; it would never be to bring me near him.

Afterward, he didn't hurry to get dressed and to get away like the others had. He stayed inside of me and I wanted him there forever. I locked my fingers into the pocket of his hip and held it tight as he finally withdrew. It was over. He would go to work in the fields and he would go to stud more slaves for Ramsey, but he would never be here; never be mine the way that I know a woman and man should be if they want to.

We belonged to Ramsey. Me, the children, this man, all of us were locked into his prison and his will. Even this feeling would be broken apart as soon as Ramsey decided that we had been in here long enough. I ached with the thought of this separation and so many separations before this one.

My ma'am had died thinking that it was just a matter of time before the gods heard her wail and returned her home. Reunited her with the world, she called it. She never believed that you could feel good right here. She had words for it in her language, but I never saw the use of making sense out of words that could not do me any good. But whatever she was saying in that old tongue, she was right.

There is no use in feeling. It will only make the days longer and the nights colder. The only resting place was far from here. The only way to keep this feeling tight inside. I must push him away. I cannot touch him. I will imagine that I am a stone, unfeeling.

I felt behind the bed until I fingered the cold blade.

As he laid on his back with that intolerable smile on his face, I plunged the metal into his chest, then touched the tip of the knife to my stomach.

I sail in a ship all around the world. I have been to the lands of snow, the islands of the sun, the great spice ridge, and to the caves where gold grows. I have been to the moon but I did not step on it. The last thing I remember before I left home was my grandfather sitting in the courtyard, watching as I diminished in the distance and asking, "Where are you going; how long will you be gone?"

I did not know. I only knew that when I returned I would be different. I would be hardened by the world.

I wrapped the cape my grandfather had given me around my shoulders and turned my back, then took my first steps into the desert.

Near the edge of the city, on the last hill before you reach the gate, I ate with an old man who treated me kindly.

He asked where I was going and I pointed in the direction which my grandfather used to point to when I asked him where we were from. Just as my grandfather would say, I said, "There."

"That is the land of famine," the old man replied.

"The land of famine," I repeated before thanking him and leaving his home.

I followed a path of no particular choosing but soon reached the place where the desert splits into the silver sands and the gold sands and the river also branches. On one side there was the soft and languid flow of the silver river, on the other was the slightly harsher movement of the gold waters. I knew that the gold desert was the home of several wild creatures and a wind controlled by demons. On the other hand, the silver desert promised to be hotter, and I did not know what its other dangers were. I did not know which to choose.

I allowed them to spread out before me into an emptiness and my eyes grew tired until all I saw was a blur of color and light. The pain of the sun on my neck subsided and my mind grew calm. The rivers separated from the blur and I chose.

It was three days before I received another drink or meal. A wrong turn. For those three days I walked across the low mountains which separated the city from its enemies to the north. For those three days I was consumed by hunger. On the third day I knew that I would die. I could feel thirst drinking my blood.

As I lay down on the third night, the skies spread before me and I was aware for the first time of their vastness. Although my father had always pointed to the heavens when he spoke of things innumerable or unknown, for the first time I felt this largeness. With no protection from the wind which swept around me, I lay helpless in the middle of the desert, staring up. All around me was silence and I stayed perfectly still, trying to learn something from the night.

I began to cry, afraid to go home, afraid of the night.

From the corners of the sands the traders surrounded me and began to babble in their ugly tongue.

By the time we reached the coast, our number had grown immeasurably, fathers, mothers, and children. Entire families. Some had sold themselves. Many of them were like me. All of us were afraid.

The motion of the waters makes me sick. My head is dizzy. Each time the waters throw the ship, bone strikes flesh. The river lifts us and drops us, like rocks in a child's hand. The wood screeches louder each time we fall. No one speaks.

Eshu, watch over us.

The sickness moves through my body. There is no warmth here. The air is heavy, I can barely inhale. Each day a few handful succumb to sickness. Their bodies are thrown overboard and the rest of us spill easily into the space which they have left behind. Before we reach the Americas, more of us will die. No one knows how many.

While the rest sleep, I slip my starved wrists from the irons and creep noiselessly into the open air. Staring into the waves, I murmur a small prayer before I cast myself over the side.

Eshu, please watch over me.

Tomas

When I was five, I went to live in the Big House. There, Master Ramsey taught me how to read. He taught all of his sons how to read. He wanted us to be gentlemen. Mrs. Ramsey did not like the idea but he was a stubborn man and once his mind was set, nothing could change it. So everyday I had lessons in reading and riding with my two brothers. However, when I reached the age of twelve, Mrs. Ramsey made such a noise about me living there that Master Ramsey was forced to send me back to the slave quarters. Before he sent me back though, he drafted the manumission papers which would grant me freedom on my twenty-first birthday.

I continued to work for him as an office boy and later as a bookkeeper, but at night I went back to the filthy huts where the slaves lived. They did not trust me, but they talked incessantly. When it behooved me, I hesitantly began to listen to their stories, thinking that they might earn me some money when I received my manumission. Now, sitting here at his desk, I wish that I had written all of their stories down and buried them deep in this earth to leave a record of the blood that flowed through here.

I will try to write an honest account now, though, for all those who perished tonight. Most of these things come from memory. Believe them. My memory gets blocked by things too painful to remember, and by those which have simply slipped away, but my heart knows the truth. As the cotton burns around me, it is all I have.

I do not know how much of it will survive but, as late as this evening, the house was a mansion. It stood in the center of the plantation facing south. Behind it there was a toolshed and storehouse. Behind these sat the slave quarters. Behind and to the sides of the slave quarters were the five thousand acres of cotton plants on which everything else was built.

The slave quarters were made of cherry wood. The finished cabins measured twelve feet by fourteen feet. The floors were red dirt packed tight by bodies. Each chimney sat five feet from the walls and was also made of wood. Although such a building was usually shared by an entire family, I was fortunate enough to occupy one alone. Master Ramsey was fond of me.

In the mornings, I rose early and stoked the small fire which burned in the stove. To this I added a pot of porridge, then read from the Bible as my meal cooked. After eating I walked, thoroughly nourished, up the slope to Ramsey's house and spent the remainder of the day logging receipts. At night I would return to my cabin and prepare another meal, then read from the Book until I fell asleep. It was a simple life.

All of this changed one night when my routine was disturbed by a visit from an old man. I had been reading but must have already fallen asleep because I do not remember him entering my cabin, so I cannot say from which direction he came. But I awoke to find him standing in my quarters waiting patiently to be acknowledged. Since it had never been my habit to interact very much with the other slaves, I did not recognize him, so unfortunately, though he is still alive, he can never be acknowledged for his good deeds. However, his face was one of the most remarkable that I have ever seen, and he stood with a pride which suggested that he was also in Ramsey's favor.

I rose and humbly offered him a seat on the bed, the only place in the room to sit. He declined. "I have come to bring you a message," he stated grandly.

What on earth could Ramsey possibly want with me at this hour, I wondered.

The stranger relayed his message, persuaded me of its merit, and left. But I spent the remainder of the night tossing in my bed and deliberating over his words.

The next day I returned to work as usual, to find that Ramsey was already in his office poring over the books.

"Didn't you sleep well last night?" he asked, noting my haggard looks.

"Why do you ask?" I inquired, a bit suspiciously in retrospect.

"You just look tired."

"No, I'm fine."

I sat down at my desk and began logging the receipts from the day before as Ramsey looked curiously at me over his shoulder.

He was generally an unassuming man who gave frequently to the usual charities and was known as a Christian to his neighbors. His outward face spoke of kindness, and indeed he was kind compared with his brethren. But I knew that he was capable of unspeakable cruelties. His eyes, his nose, his mouth, all of them were the same as my own.

Only two days earlier I had come into my majority, and to mark the occasion, he made a lengthy speech about the value of my service to the plantation on the one hand, while with the other, he delayed my manumission. Strange that I should think of this now, but I remembered how he had taken me to live in his home. Singling me out, supposedly because of my advanced intelligence, he said that he intended to educate me. In those days he was jovial and warm and I felt safe when he was near me. I had not yet learned the fear of adults.

For years he was my mentor and everything like a father, but later he would break under his wife's jealousy and I would never be so close to him as I had been as a child, when it had been permissible for him to pull me affectionately close and to whisper a knowing word into my ear. It was our secret. No one had thought anything of it. I was only a child. But as I grew, I began to resemble him suspiciously, in the minds of those around us, and as my shoulders grew defiant I thought nothing of the way I acted around the white people or the slaves.

One day I overheard him speaking to Mrs. Ramsey. From the edge of the doorway, I saw her standing over him as he sat in his favorite chair. At first she seemed remarkably calm. "The way you treat that darkie, one would think he was your own flesh and blood." My stomach climbed to my throat as I waited for his response. Ramsey remained silent and she continued. "I mean, the idea of it, William, teaching him how to read. What kind of thoughts are you trying to put in his head anyway?"

She waited for his answer, but when no reply came, she pounced on him. With one hand she snatched the paper that he had been pretending to read, while clawing at his face with her other one. "I know the truth, William," she screamed as Ramsey tried to protect his face and grab her hands at the same time.

"What truth?" he finally asked her.

"You cavorting with that, that whore, is one thing, but how dare you insult me by having him live in this house?"

"What are you talking about?" Ramsey demanded.

"William, I know," she said in a pained voice. "The darkies know it too. I heard them talking about it in the kitchen. I want that nigger out of my house."

Ramsey got up and walked toward the door to close it. Still undiscovered, I ran crying to my room.

The next day, I was sent to live with the slaves. After that, there would be no chance of ever touching him as my brothers George and Robert did; no chance of me ever knowing him the way I had when I was small and he had led me to believe in that closeness.

As I thought of this, I met the man's stare with resentfulness, and he turned away while I resumed working. We spent the remainder of the day in an awkward silence.

When I returned to the slave quarters that evening, I did not go directly home, but stopped at the cabin where Casby lived. Casby was an old man who had been purchased when he was twelve years old. His wife had died five years earlier and he had not spoken since she passed away. No one knew whether this condition was caused by his grief or the stubbornness of old age.

I entered his room and was immediately overcome by the putrid smell. It reminded me of the smell from the slaves' outhouse, which I refused to use.

Casby said nothing but looked at me hard, studying everything that I did. As I spoke he nodded as if he had already had this conversation and knew exactly what I would say before the words left my tongue, as though meaning was not in them but in my movements.

I labored to keep a straight face as I wrestled with the smell of the room and the sight of this filthy old man. Finally, I completed delivery of the message which I had received the previous evening. He then looked back at me and a long creaky sound came from his mouth, like a door that had not been opened for too long a time. "I knew that you would come tonight," he said. Then he stood up and hugged me, squeezing my body into his own filthy being. I left his cabin and ran back to my own, sucking deeply on the crisp air. When I finally reached my cabin I read for a short time from the Book before falling asleep.

The next morning as I went to work, I saw Ramsey, at the top of the slope, talking to an evil-looking man and pointing toward the swamps. When I approached, they suddenly stopped talking and the man gave me a scrutinizing glance. My heart quickened until Ramsey said, "He's all right, one of my best." He winked at me after saying this, then beckoned me into his office. Inside he told me that there had been a runaway last night. He asked me to be his spy in the slave quarters. I quickly agreed because I relished the uncertain irony of the situation.

I left his office and returned to my books. Because Ramsey was caught up in the business of Casby there was not much to do and I finished the day's work by noon. I then asked him for the remainder of the afternoon off. He granted it, and I left, intending to go for a walk to enjoy the beauty of the country.

When I reached the birch behind the slave cabins, in the little field before you reach the cotton rows, I sat down. It was there that my mind began to reluctantly scrutinize my actions.

I felt an uncertain imbroglio of emotion, but more than anything, I sensed that I was an unwilling player in a game crafted by others.

I thought back to the shame which engulfed me when I first returned to live with the slaves and the humiliation which I had suffered from Mrs. Ramsey. My entire existence had been controlled by the commands and opinions of those around me. It was not as it was with the other slaves, who were told when to perform all of their daily actions, but the unique torture of a purgatory in which I was unable to locate myself.

I turned to the thought of Casby as he headed north and my body filled with rage. Why should such a worthless being have freedom while I continued to suffer the humiliation of my present condition? He would not know what to do with freedom because he had never known it. As a child I had felt what it was like to move according to my own desire.

I had risked my life for something as foul as he and with no reward to myself. I had heard reports that Negroes less fair-skinned than I, and with little to no education, made quite handsome livings for themselves in the cities of the North. Why not? I knew of some here who had their own slaves, and not one of them was my equal. Why did I have to suffer being Ramsey's bastard?

I knew that I could leave by the same route which carried Casby, but I also knew that if caught the punishment would be unbearable. Besides, my freedom would come in a short time. I would wait patiently. In the meantime I would help those I could, the ones with nothing to wait for.

I listened again to the voice which had brought me the message, and something in me began to stir. It was then that I was filled with happiness and a perfect lucidity of mind. Perhaps He had chosen me to be His messenger. What higher calling could there be? Even as a child I had had the strange feeling that I was meant for something beyond my station as a captive. It was not an idealistic slave but an angel in my cabin. Yes, I had been set apart.

I fell asleep with this feeling. When I awoke, the night had grown thick around me. I rose and made my way back to the slave quarters.

When I arrived, smoke poured from the chimneys of the huts, and the smell of boiling cabbage made my stomach stir. Instead of going to my own cabin as usual, I mustered the courage to knock on the door next to mine. The woman who opened it was the seamstress, Caroline. She eyed me suspiciously, but when I told her that it was too late for me to cook she invited me in.

I sat on the floor with her two filthy children as she brought us corn bread and molasses with the cabbage and some bacon, which she had probably taken from the kitchen. After we ate, she sent the children to sleep. As I searched for something to say, she stared at me through the smoky room. Uneasily, I began to get up.

"You did it, didn't you?" she said as I pulled myself from the floor.

"Did what?"

"Helped Casby get away."

"I don't know what you're talking about."

"You showed him how to get on the Train," she insisted.

"No."

"But no one else could have. I won't tell. I told them you wasn't all bad."

"Told who?" I asked nervously.

"The others."

"They think I am?" As I asked this question, I immediately regretted it. They could not possibly have any other opinion of me, especially those who knew that I was his son.

"Just some. You know how . . ." She stumbled for words that would not offend me too greatly. Then finally she said, "I want you to help us."

I walked toward the door and thanked her for the meal. "I don't know what you're talking about," I answered curtly, and before she could reply, I walked out of her cabin and headed briskly toward home.

Once there, my head strained with fear as I leaned against my closed door. The buoyancy of my earlier happiness dissipated and I was left with nothing but the weight of what I had done: If a woman as simple as Caroline had figured out that I was responsible, surely Ramsey also knew. When I fell asleep, I dreamed of her and her children. Picnicking in a field, they were dressed in starched white cloth. When I approached them, they hurriedly packed their food away and began to run. I woke up in the middle of the night choked by the stillness of the air.

No one else had ever shown me kindness except Ramsey, and he was not even fit to wear the clothes which she sewed. She deserved better; her children deserved better.

My own mother had died in this foul place and she had not even received a wooden cross to mark the spot where she rested. When I returned to live in the slave quarters she had approached me and said, "Welcome my baby home." The shame of her life had led me to pretend I did not know her and to feign forgetfulness. "Who are you?" I asked.

The woman replied, "Your mother," then turned haughtily and left. I had delivered to her the worst insult a child can give. She had wanted to hold me, to have someone to care for, but bitterness caused her to deny this and all other emotions. He had already used her and driven her into the ground and all she wanted was the warmth of her blood in her cabin at night. I had denied her that and left her to die with strange men and knives and God only knows what else in her sinful shack. Think whatever you will about me, but also know that as I thought about it that night, I fell to my knees and prayed for forgiveness.

In the morning I heard the sounds of the workers heading into the fields as I turned groggily in my bed. I rubbed the half sleep from my eyes to see the heavy sun rise, a beautiful almond with honey edges. As it moved, it grew brighter, pushing the sky up with it. I watched as the line of people walking toward the fields, and the sky turning through its motions. They moved beneath it, unaware of the beauty above them. I had already decided that I would help Caroline, but it was only then that I resolved to help all of us. All of them, my blood.

When I reported to work that morning, I told

Ramsey that I had heard some of the slaves were stealing from the kitchen. This I did to confuse him by satisfying my role as spy. When he pressed me, I told him it was Caroline.

When the slaves returned from the fields, he had her taken to the toolshed and beaten so that the other slaves could hear the screams.

The following week I returned to Caroline's, where I found one of the children rubbing fat onto the wounds left from her beating. I felt responsible but knew that it was a small price for her to pay for freedom. I did not mention that I was involved.

As I told her in exact detail the route which she would have to follow, she thanked me profusely as tears formed in her eyes, swelled to fullness, then finally ran down her face.

"Why are you crying?" I asked dumbly.

"I'm crying for you, baby. You so confused. I wish I could help you the way you done for us but I can't." My only reply was to tell her that I was not confused in the slightest. Another lie.

She looked at me for a second, then went behind the stove and came back with a small gold loop.

"What's that?" I asked incredulously, eyeing the metal as she pushed it into my hand.

"It's for you. My mamma got it from a trader who got it from her home." I stared at her in confusion.

"From over the water."

I looked at her, not knowing what to say, then took the small piece of metal and placed it in my pocket. On the way home, I would finger it through the material of my trousers to make sure that it was still there. I had never known that anything beautiful could come from Africa.

They found her body by the river. The children escaped though. Only God knows how.

They buried the body where they found it, but the bounty hunter brought back the head so that Ramsey could identify it. Even Ramsey found this gesture too grotesque to bear. He looked contemptuously at the man as he paid him, then silently dismissed him from the room.

I did not see the head but I am sure it affected him greatly, because Father has denied me my freedom again. He said that my general behavior since returning to the slave quarters had been atavistic. However, he was willing to give me one more chance to improve upon my character. He said that I would be free upon his death, pending proof of my loyalty and moral character to the executor of his estate. That is all he said.

There could be no doubt then that he suspected I had been aiding the escapes. It did not matter. God had given me a vision. Neither Ramsey nor any other man could stop it.

I spent my days working as before. Ramsey, however, had assigned me a new task. Claiming that I would be of more use elsewhere, he removed me from the office and placed me in charge of the stables and the kennels, where he kept his hunting dogs. The work was monotonous and strenuous but it afforded me an opportunity to have more contact with the other slaves. I performed the work diligently, endlessly patient.

In the evenings I began to eat with the other slaves on a regular basis and everyone seemed happy to have my company among them. If they remembered what I was like before, they did not mention it. After eating we sat around the fire and told stories. The old people were full of tales about spirits and things too hard to say. But beneath our laughter there was always an unacknowledged heaviness. Looking into the eyes around the fire, you could always find a moistness, like dew clinging to a darkness too far away to shelter it from the sun.

On Sundays we congregated in a small clearing and the faithful gave thanks. It was not like the church in town, where I sat in the back as the white preacher offered dry words to the flock and paltry praise to the Lord. In the clearing Brother Gabe always led us with a fiery sermon and we responded with living voices. At first I found this mayhem disconcerting, but after only a short time I could not believe that I had missed this jubilee for so many years. It was like praying to a different god.

Sunday, always a welcome respite, had become my only release from the tensions of the week, which seemed ready to break at any moment. After Caroline's escape, Ramsey was intent on finding a scapegoat. He had been unhappy enough to call a bounty hunter to pursue Casby but he knew that the old man was of no value to him. Besides, he had probably died in the wilderness. Caroline, though, was skilled and valuable. He needed to set an example for the rest of us. No one spoke of this.

Finally Ramsey chose Caleb, a notoriously rebellious worker. On the appointed morning the overseer took Caleb down to the birch and placed a rope around his neck. He then called all of the slaves out to the tree and interrogated Caleb in front of us.

"Which way did you tell them to go?" Ramsey shouted more than asked.

"I didn't tell them nothing," Caleb spat back.

"I'm only going to ask you this last time," Ramsey said. "So you can cleanse your mind before the Lord."

"I ain't did nothing," Caleb insisted. He might have looked slightly defiant but for the rope around his neck.

On and on they went through these motions. Caleb held fast, refusing to give a false confession. Blow after blow fell on the man's back. You could tell that he was straining not to break as his voice started to tremble before the inevitable. You never seen nothing like the way they beat that nigger down. You never dreamed nothing like the way he wouldn't cry. Cow whip crushing down on his backside, blood running loose and free. No tears, just the veins showing through the skin on his face, and his lips trembling, trying to mouth something. Not one word got through, only the sound of his life running to meet its heaven.

The others tried to avert their eyes. No one dared

breathe for fear of adding wind to the sails of death, until from the other side of the circle a voice called out.

It was Paul, one of the boys that Ramsey had bought down in the Caribbean. I could not understand what he was saying, but some of the old people shouted and began to cry. Susan rushed forth and tried to scoop the boy up, but she could not move him. He was heavy with anger. The overseer hesitated and the pandemonium grew louder.

Ramsey's eyes locked with Caleb's and, as the confusion around them soared, they continued to exchange stares.

Finally Ramsey fired the gun, which sent the horse flying, left the trapdoor swinging, and Caleb hanging for my crimes. I vomited. Ramsey gave me a knowing look, which I met before going back to my cabin.

Still, I continued to help our people escape. Even Caleb's death could not deter me. Although he and Caroline had been sacrificed, they were only two. Their deaths, though painful, did not measure against the dozens of others who had slipped quietly into the world.

Instead of sending these hopefuls north as I had before, I began directing them south to an Indian reservation, where I was guaranteed that they would receive shelter. But I was not satisfied with the prospect of mere shelter. A handful of escapes, scattered over months, was not enough. I developed a plan.

What had begun as a frightening message had grown to obsess me. I spent all of my waking hours making contact with those who believed as I did and all of my sleeping ones dreaming of our victory. Ramsey still did not know for certain who was betraying him, but I was sure that I would be his next victim. Slowly, I began to put my plan into action.

Guns, picks, axes, anything which could be used to kill suddenly began to fall into disrepair and had to be replaced, until we had amassed a small arsenal at Ramsey's expense. I dug a hole in the dirt of my cabin floor and stored the weapons.

The fortnight following Caleb's death, I accompanied Ramsey to New Orleans so that he could purchase a few new slaves. When he asked me to accompany him, I thought briefly that our relations were beginning to thaw. However, when we reached the city, I quickly realized that he wanted only to inflict more pain by making me watch the horrible proceedings, as if he were saying, "You may save a couple, but I can replace them tenfold." The stream of bodies pouring into that wicked city from the far side of the ocean seemed boundless. I saw them being marched through the street like a black tide without beginning or end.

On the Sunday following our arrival, we went to a bricked area in a large pasture which the natives called Congo Square for obvious reasons. The area around the square was thronged by those seeking to purchase and by the merely curious. In the middle, a hundred or so Africans cowered as an auctioneer lied about their merits.

Unable to watch the proceedings, I wandered through the crowd. Ramsey knew that he held the prospect of legitimate freedom over my head and never seemed to worry about me escaping. He never even looked up to see where I was going. Among the crowd I met a freeman from Brazil who had bought his contract out and was returning to his native Angola. He was traveling on an empty slaver that had stopped here so that its crew might enjoy the debauchery of the place before fulfilling its journey. Through one of the crew members, who acted as interpreter, he spoke to me of his bondage in Brazil, but he spent the majority of his time telling me about his native land. I was envious of him, even though I firmly believed that the future for us was here.

Two days after our return Master Ramsey died, owing to a great misfortune while hunting. I would finally be free. I did not know what I would do when I set foot into the world, but my mind took both pleasure and pain poring over the possibilities.

I was quickly relieved of my quandary because the executor of Ramsey's estate, his oldest son, George, refused to grant me the freedom which had been promised by our father. This came as no surprise. Even as a child, George had been unspeakably wicked. He had inherited none of that small parcel of humanity Ramsey once possessed.

I remember him taking great pleasure in torturing the smallest of the slave girls. He had always been especially jealous of me because I had outperformed him during our studies. No, I was not surprised. I also suspected that he would kill me before

I could carry out my plan. The thought of abandoning the other slaves filled me with pain, but I could not allow myself to be the victim of George's taste for violence.

I had been patient; now it was time for me to be wise.

Dressed as a woman, I left my cabin. The skirt was nothing more than a rag, but a woman, no matter how she is dressed, is less suspicious than a man. Under my skirt I wore my own pants and had hidden a parcel of food. I crept down the road to the edge of the cotton and began to find my way through the rows of plants. When I reached the clearing I ran furiously toward the swamps. The marsh and its woods were unfamiliar and I was surrounded by the awful noises of the night and wished for my porridge and for my bed.

I ran with nothing but the North Star to guide me. I kept moving until my legs locked beneath me, refusing to go on. I could not stop though. I knew that there was an abandoned cabin nearby. It was the same cabin that I directed the runaways to. As I searched for the building, my thoughts grew incoherent. My mind grew delirious and I began to imagine the ghosts of those whom I knew had died while trying to escape.

My fingers wouldn't move right. They couldn't hold on like they used to. Before, even when I didn't want them to hold they did. Reaching out to log the name of another purchase, no matter how hard I swore that I would not. Pushing out to push my mother away, no matter how hard I told them that this was their mother too. And sloshing against water when my mind told them that it was time to stop, no getting away. The stranger, he didn't tell me about the cold. He just said to be at the swamp and wait for a signal; he didn't say my hands would freeze up. So many sins on these hands, it's no wonder they didn't want to move, even if it was their first time to move without being told what to do by somebody. All that freedom and my hands couldn't move to touch it.

Caroline appeared with her head tied in a white cloth and silently she directed me. The swampy ground caved in beneath my weight, but I trudged on, following a woman whom I knew was not there and all the time feeling that I had made this journey before.

As the moon began to set, I finally saw the cabin. Caroline whispered something to me in a language that I did not understand. Only one word made itself heard before she vanished and I collapsed onto the doorway of the building.

In the morning I heard the dogs. A trail of fear had brought them.

I extinguished the fire in the stove, then opened the door and breathed in what I thought would be my last breath. I ran.

The water was only three miles away. A cruel joke. I raced toward it as the dogs' barking grew louder. My side tightened and my chest began to heave laboriously. I would not make it. I headed deeper into the wilderness; the dogs gained ground. I felt the earth tremble with their weight. There was no escape. I climbed a large tree and waited.

When they came, I lay impossibly still, hoping against hope that they would turn around. The dogs stopped at the tree, barking victoriously as they ran around its trunk. More than my own life, I wanted to kill them, to pounce from my perch and grab one of them by the neck while the others devoured me. I lay still. The men were not far away. Their voices

cut through the air and their guns rang out to cele-
brate the end of the chase. My heart rose to my
throat and cut off my breathing. As I struggled for
air, I tasted my own saliva mixed with the tepid
blood of fear.

With my last breath, I dropped from the branch
and grabbed the nearest dog; the rest pounced on me
but I held the dog's neck like life, robbing him of
breath. I felt the blood seeping from my arms, my
legs, my heart. It ran loose and free. It ran free. I did
not feel.

When I awoke, I saw his face. It was the same
bounty hunter who had spoken to Ramsey after
Casby ran. He watched me stir, then came over to
me and kicked my rib cage. There was a snap and I
passed out again. When I awoke I heard their voices.
"Dumb nigger, cost us our best dog."

A smile passed inside me. Only a small one. At
least I had taken something from them.

"Nigger must be crazy, never seen nothing like it.
We should put a leash around his neck. Never seen
a beast do what that crazy nigger just done."

He noticed me stirring and walked over to my
sprawled form. A small stream of spittle formed on
his bottom lip and hung in the light, collecting force
before it fell toward me. I struggled to move out of
its way. My body did not respond. I lay motionless
as his saliva collected in the sockets of my eyes, then
streamed down my face. I began to cry with rage.

He smiled with pleasure at this, then pushed me
onto my stomach with the toe of his muddied boot.
I felt his weight upon me. I clutched my pocket,
searching for Caroline's ring. It was gone. My pock-
ets were gone. I was naked on the floor and his cruel
weight fell on my back. With a voice that sounded
capable of anything, he whispered in my ear, "You

gone like this, boy." I stared at the fading kerosene lamp as he entered me.

I awoke as we turned onto the road leading to the Ramsey plantation. Several young children stopped their playing, stared at me, and ran off into the fields. Afraid. When we got to George Ramsey's study, my brother looked up at me and his eyes glistened. I locked on to them and he turned away. He then called for an overseer and had me taken to the barn, where I was locked up. Later George came in, whip in hand. This he gave to the overseer and stepped back a pace.

I had never suffered the lash before. When it fell on me, its cruelness cut my back and I trembled with agony. Each time the hide found my flesh though, I spit out the word "brother," unafraid. The louder I screamed this, the harder the whip fell, until the overseer was exhausted.

"Won't do no good. Can't whip a dead man," George said, stopping the overseer's fury. They walked out of the barn and I was left alone.

At night the women and children brought me food. Each evening after they left the fields a different one came in to gawk or give sympathy. It was all the same. Four nights ago Dorothy, a girl of about eighteen, came in with hot porridge mixed with honey. My mouth opened to take the food without saying anything. She, in turn, did not speak to me. She simply spooned the stuff into my mouth and I swallowed without tasting it. My eyes locked on to hers as the food passed down my throat, and she stared back unflinching, looking into me with hatred.

The next night she came again. In this way we established a routine. She brought my food and I stared at her. She was a strong woman, unmoved by my eyes or my condition. I remembered she could pick almost two hundred pounds a day, as much as any man, but her body was frail and her eyes hollow, her hands heavy with scars and veins. She caught me staring at them and finally spoke to me. "I guess you never had to work in the fields. You thought you was special. The way you walked around here. Looking at us like dogs; meaner than all of them white folks put together. Then come to think you some kind of savior or something. Well, I guess they learned you. You just like the rest of us."

I knew that she was saying the truth. It hurts to think that I was once so completely lost, but I swallowed and continued to stare at her. I struggled to maintain my composure but my pain leaked through, compelling her to soften.

"I guess you did get some out though." She spooned another spoonful of stuff into my mouth, then wiped my face with a cloth and turned to leave.

"Help me," I said, almost whispering.

"Help you what. You can't go nowhere like this."

"You his spy?"

"No. I ain't a spy, but if you leave here you'll be dead before you reach the road, that's all."

"Guns."

"What?"

I told her my plan. She left. Either she would betray me or join me. I had no control over it. A peace settled over me. Live or die. It was simple. I said a small prayer as I fell asleep. The next night she brought me a slice of cake with my porridge, either a good omen or my last meal. It no longer mattered.

"I told them."

My heart quickened; I had been betrayed. I smiled and began to laugh. They could do me no more harm.

"Hush up," she said. "They scared. Real scared, but

they said okay." After saying this she turned to leave and I mouthed a barely audible thank you, meant neither for her nor myself.

Last night a small boy came in with my food. I thought that perhaps Dorothy had been discovered and was now locked up in her own prison. Perhaps she was also without fear because she knew.

"Ramsey say he going to let you loose."

"What?" I asked.

"I was playing around the white folk and I hear Ramsey say he going to let you loose."

"What else did you hear?"

"That's all he said, just that he couldn't do nothing about it except let you go."

I thought about this for the rest of the night. I knew that it was too simple. He could do whatever he wanted to me; letting me go was too easy. Either the boy had misheard or George was planning something else. I could not trust it. The only thought which quieted my mind was knowing that if anything happened to me Dorothy would carry out the plan.

This morning, George walked in. Pushing the barrel of his hunting rifle into my neck, he unlocked my chains. His hand went up in a threatening gesture. I moved to block with the same hand. His eyes bore into me with hatred. I stared back at him with the same eyes until he withdrew his rifle and stepped back. Then he turned around passionately, swinging the butt of the gun into the side of my face. I felt the bones collapse and the flesh cave in. Falling into a heap on the ground I clutched the side of my face. He grabbed my neck, and pushed my head into the ground.

"I want you gone," he screamed into the top of my head. "If it wasn't for my daddy's will, I would kill you." Then for emphasis, "I would've killed you a long time ago."

I lifted my head to say something. Only to have it shoved down again.

"I suggest you get as far away from here as your nigger legs will carry you."

He left and I walked painfully down to the cabins. Inside, I clawed at the dirt around the stove. Maybe they were buried deeper than I remembered. I got a shovel and anxiously turned over the dirt of my floor. Nothing.

My weapons were gone. He had found them. How could I think that they would still be there? As I sat against the cold stove clutching my face, Dorothy came in.

"You wanted us to leave the stuff here until Ramsey found it. We ain't stupid."

I jumped up and snatched her arm to pull her to me.

"They just waiting for the signal," she said as she turned and left. I went to the bed and searched around until I found the Book. I read from it until I began to fall asleep. I was awakened by the shouting from the meeting place. I climbed out of bed and hurried down.

At the stump near the water Brother Gabe was yelling and praying like I never seen. When he saw me, all the shouting stopped and he smiled before starting up again even louder than he had been. How we shouted tonight. I found my body fill with a new strength, like the strength I had when I killed the dog; but without anger, without fear. I began to dance, until all around me bodies moved and became possessed by the goodness. We ate until there was no more food. We then returned to our cabins and I laid in my bed waiting for the bottomless darkness. When the night was finally deep around me, I gave the signal and the entire sky lit up.

The cotton burned beautifully.

While the others were setting fire to the fields I walked slowly to the main house with a deliberate smile. Inside I found George as he was dressing to join the neighbors who had already come in droves. As I entered the house I heard the word which I imagined Caroline had spoken in the swamp, repeated over and over like a prayer. I steeled my mind though, refusing to let any thoughts through. Without emotion, I crept behind him and circled his warm throat with cold hands. When they find me the soul will have already left my body, and when they hang the body, I will keep my eyes open, staring at them until the flesh falls away and the blood of this place is finally quiet. I killed my brother, like a dog.

I remember. High in the night sky there is a trapeze which lovers swing on. The ropes are made by Ursa Major and its Minor. The handle is the horizontal plane of the Southern Cross.

Their movements are not controlled by them. They merely respond to physics. The same laws which form gravity and light make their bodies move. Their hearts quicken and their brains release endorphins. Their pupils dilate. They do not know that this is happening to them. They only know that they are flying.

And they swing in the air, performing impossible somersaults and always catching each other. They smile, knowing that they are beautiful and frightening to watch. The North Star lights the spectacle.

Lying on my back in the Southern Hemisphere, I have seen this trapeze, barely visible above the horizon. She swings him and he releases her hands to turn a blood-freezing spin. Turning, turning, turning. She catches him at the ankles and they swing on, smiling at each other. This is what they know. They are flying.

They do not know that gravity will eventually pull them down. But when they finally fall to the earth, they will laugh and hold each other. They will breathe effortlessly in rhythm. You can only breathe with the same rhythm as someone else for so long.

Under rain clouds in the Northern Hemisphere, I have ridden this trapeze.

I remember.

Somewhere on my journey I met a woman who sang for the sun and danced for the moon. Her magic was more powerful than mine, she moved through time, but she did not know my name and our love did not last.

It was the highest point in the city. Grass stretched up and the jarring noise of the streets was only a faraway hum.

I sat perfectly still as she read my palm. I did not hear her words, only the sound of her voice as she traced: lifeline, moneyline, loveline. Later we would fight or be apart and ache for each other. For now though, we melt into the grass and coo like imbeciles. We kiss, two lovers on the top of a hill. If people down below can see us, that is what they say, pointing up with their mouths open. Two lovers on top of a hill.

Antoinette

Me, Ezra, and Mamma was all hid in a tunnel behind the wall of the cabin when light flashed between the slits in the board and a man called out Mamma's name. She sloshed through the muddy water and went out to meet him, but she had presence of mind to make me and Ezra stay behind. The last thing I heard was Mamma's scream against the flat night. She never came back.

I don't know how long we stayed hid. But I know that when a second light cut through the dark, I dragged in a breath deep enough to hold until morning. But by the time I rushed over to cover his mouth it was too late.

Ezra screamed out "Mamma" as loud as he could, and when the boards gave way, the only thing you could see was the shadow of a gun spread across the wall. You didn't need to see the man behind it.

Me and Ezra both started crying. I know I should have known better, but I couldn't help it. I screamed just as loud as the baby.

The man didn't hurt us though, he just said to hush up. When he stepped down into the tunnel, I could see that he was a black man. You couldn't hardly tell, but the slight yellow of his skin and soft swell of his lips was enough. After I saw that, I wasn't worried too much. I knew we would be mostly safe.

He picked Ezra up and carried him piggyback outside to the waiting carriage.

Years later, when he proposed to me, that was the image that stuck in my head. I didn't think about what I had found out since then, the drinking and the strings of women he had run through, I just thought about how gentle he had been with my little brother.

By the time we got in front of the preacherman, it took all the strength I had to say yes a second time. In the four months between when he bent down on his knee for me and when I walked between the chairs set up in Miss Harris's living room, we had already started to fight so much that I knew I had nothing to look forward to but 'til-death-do-us-part misery. For the first time, I was happy that he was nearly twenty years older than me and not a young man who would live just as long as I would.

Maybe it wasn't him at all, just the way men turn after they get what they after. But I didn't have anything to compare him to except Jeremiah, and I hadn't waited long enough to see which way he would turn.

Jeremiah was Mr. Wilkes's youngest boy and handsome for a dark-skinned man. But even though his family had lived up here for, they said, two generations, they didn't have much money. He was a hard worker though, and a gentle man. I remember the Sunday he first asked me out. There was a circus in town and folks couldn't wait to get out of church and go look at all that foolishness. He walked up to me as me and Ezra was leaving and asked if I'd like to go with him. Jeremiah was two shades darker than the night, but I swear to God he blushed when he asked me. Inside, I trembled with a warmth but I had to tell him no. There was nobody to take care of Ezra, and even though he was a grown man, I still worried about leaving him alone.

I guess I gave him a little smile or something to encourage him, because every week after that, a month of Sundays, he asked me out until I didn't have any excuses left.

His sister came to look after Ezra while me and Jeremiah went to the pictures. Even though I think he was a bit jealous, Ezra flashed me a smile when I looked back at him before leaving the house.

"You sure love that boy," Jeremiah said after we had walked a few blocks and ran out of things to say about the weather.

"Who? Oh, you mean Ezra. Well, that's all the family I got," I told him.

He looked down at the sidewalk, almost guilty. I don't know how much he knew, but the people in the church was full of gossip about me and Ezra. Damn hypocrites, it was all I could do to see the Holy Ghost between all those devilish heads talking about what God like and what He don't on a Sunday morning. I almost walked out of the church forever when the preacher with his uppity self looked straight at me and said, "God don't like no bastard child." I don't know who he thought he was, but

49

ain't no God I ever heard of kicked nobody out of heaven 'cause his mamma and daddy wasn't married. If He did, though, the preacher was better off worrying about that boy they said he had with Rose. They were all just mad that instead of testifying, I sat in the back every Sunday keeping my business between me and God.

"My mamma was a slave," I told him. "She died trying to bring me and my brother to freedom." That shut him up. But suddenly I didn't want him to be shut up anymore. His iron-black eyes fell to the ground again like I had slapped them and the boyishness made me want to see what was behind them. I wanted to know how red was his heart. But it was too late. The crowd of people leaving the last show began to push around us and I knew there wouldn't be another chance to talk until we left and headed home.

The first time I went to the pictures was with Lily. She used to be a dancer in one of the theaters downtown. But she got pregnant and stopped dancing. Right after the baby was born she got left by the man who made her pregnant. She said he told her he wasn't the marrying type of man and I guess to prove just what kind of man he was, he abandoned Lily and their three-month-old baby, Alice.

One by one she sold all her possessions, until all she had left was her child. Finally, she sold the girl too. Folks said that's how she ended up in the nigger part of town, 'cause only a nigger could do something like that.

But Lily didn't keep a ledger with her daughter's name and how many pieces of silver she fetched, neither did any of the colored people I knew.

She used to go down to the picture show to watch the light dance across the screen in the dark room.

She said it was soothing. The ladies in the pictures didn't remind her of anything.

When I went with her I felt the same way. The way she taught me to watch them, we didn't even remember we were sitting next to each other until the lights came back up. But sitting with Jeremiah was exactly the opposite. I couldn't forget he was next to me and my head raced with memories I wanted to tell him about and when the lights came on I was already thinking about the kiss he would try to give me when we said goodnight.

When we got outside though, everything I wanted to tell him about was forgotten. We talked for a little while about the show, but then the words started to dry up again, like blood in open air, until we were standing in front of my house. We had already walked up the first stone step in silence when he circled his arm around my waist and pulled me toward him. I turned my head to see if anyone was looking, then gave him the briefest peck on the lips before slipping out of his hold and running up the stairs.

When I walked into the living room, Ezra and Jeremiah's sister were both asleep on the couch. I woke her silently and told her that Jeremiah was waiting downstairs to walk her home, then I made sure to thank her before shutting the door.

After she was gone I checked on Ezra to see if he was still asleep, then put a blanket over him and went down the hall to the other room.

Just as I laid down to sleep there was the light tap of a pebble on the window. I pulled on my robe and walked over, making sure I couldn't be seen from below. I was expecting to see Jeremiah standing down there and I still hadn't decided what I would do if he was. Instead, I saw Lily leaning against the fence in her housecoat. I turned the light on and opened the window. "Come around back," I whispered to her, then fumbled around the room to find the key.

"What are you doing out so late?" I asked Lily, taking her elbow and pulling her inside.

"You didn't tell me you had a date tonight," she said as we slipped up the stairs.

"You woke me up for that?" I asked her. But she was grinning like a safecracker. We went into the kitchen and I put a pot of tea on, then picked up some back orders that I hadn't finished.

"Here," I said, handing her a pile of cotton shirts, "as long as you got me up you might as well help with some of this work."

We spent the next few hours sewing and gossiping like little girls, and by the time Lily finished picking my brain, we could hear the milk cart coming up the street.

"You might as well sleep here," I said. "You know how people are." They were already full of gossip about this house. Let them talk. As far as I was concerned wasn't nothing going on here worse than what they was doing. They thought they knew something about my life, but if they knew what I did, they would keep their mouths shut.

You could tell everything about a person from who wore linen and who wore cotton, and who had a blouse made out of the same material as somebody else's wife, and what kind of stains all of them had.

As I pulled the covers around us, Lily asked me if I was thinking about marriage. I told her not to even start on that and kissed her good night. But the truth was that I wasn't getting any younger and it was getting harder and harder to keep food in the cupboard and stitches on two backs. Ezra had tried to find work a couple of times, but the factories was too dangerous for him. In the spring he would do a little gardening, but that never gave him more than a few pennies to spend. Besides, I had never been married and hadn't ever had a little girl.

I tucked my arm under Lily's head and kissed the back of her neck, pressing my face into the sweetness of her hair, then fell asleep.

When I woke up Lily had already left and the sun was midway through the sky. I washed and went to the kitchen, where Ezra was sitting finishing the sewing me and Lily had started the night before. I gave him a smile, then went across the room and started sifting the flour to make biscuits.

It was the end of August and the air was turning fresh as truth and pure as a promise that wouldn't break. Just behind though, you could feel the white teeth of winter and the call for warm coats and full buckets of coal. I could only hope that the business coming in now would be enough to carry us through the lean months and into the hard-to-get spring.

It was too much to think about though. I pushed the kitchen window open wider to let the last warm winds in. But a quick gust carried the shirt Ezra was sewing over his head and he snatched at it like a clumsy kitten until he could see again. When he had smoothed the material back out, Ezra rolled his eyes at me with a sideways tilt of the head that I could only laugh at.

I gave a shrug before walking over to the oven and taking the biscuits out. Ezra put the shirt aside and broke one of them open before it had time to cool, sopping up the syrup with one half before putting it in his mouth. He nodded his head and gave me an approving look, then did the same thing with the other half. I watched the top of his head as he ate noiselessly and wondered what went on inside during the endless quiet hours.

I don't know how long it was before I first noticed it. Two days? Three? I know that for the rest of the trip up here he was quiet as a church on Mardi Gras, and I thought he was just overwhelmed by the terror of leaving home. But three days passed, then four, then five. I shook him and yelled and dropped things to get his attention but nothing I did could penetrate his silence. Calling out Mamma's name had been the last thing I'd heard my brother say, and my whispered voice, telling him to hush up, seemed to be the last thing he ever heard.

Years had gone by until I couldn't remember him any other way. I forgot what his voice sounded like, I think, at the same time that I searched my memory for a picture of Mamma and couldn't bring nothing up except gray mist.

But by and by we found new ways to talk to each other. Smiles and frowns and hugs and light touches and hand signals could get across even the most complicated ideas. Mainly, though, we became expert at reading each other's face until I hardly noticed the absence of words when we were alone. So used to it that I found myself passing whole weeks without uttering a sound and without wishing for any other company.

We would sit the entire afternoon sewing quilts and blankets like the ones Mamma made, and the colors and patterns turned into conversations and stories better than any words because you could touch them with your fingers to trace a thread of thought and it couldn't lie.

We were living in Miss Harris's two back rooms

then and making the quilts out of the few scraps of cloth she would let us have to play with. But when she saw what we were making, she said folks would pay good money if we sewed them out of real material and took us to Colber's, where there were rows and rows of fabric. More than I had ever seen in my life and me and Ezra took a whole day just to touch them and I learned the name of everything from old Colber. Finally we took three yards of purple cambric and four yards of white chenille and an armful of odds and ends that Colber put in for free.

It took four weeks to finish the quilt but when it was done Miss Harris sold it to one of the women from church and we took the money to buy more materials. At first we were so happy for the money we were getting that we didn't think of nothing else except what kinds of designs to make and the next trip to Colber's. But after a while, it started getting depressing to see strangers come in and take away something we had worked so hard on. We started spending longer and longer on each quilt until folks threatened to take their orders back. When they saw what we made for them though—piousness for a baptism and cheerfulness for a birthday or luck for a wedding—their eyes always brightened and we probably could have gotten twice what they were paying.

After a while we had saved up enough money, and gotten old enough, to move out of Miss Harris's and rent an apartment of our own. When we moved in, the first thing we decided to do was to stop making quilts and just sew shirts and the like, things that we didn't feel any attachment to. To make up for the money we lost, we took in some cleaning from time to time—only when the snow piled higher than usual and you couldn't see the end of winter, and didn't know how much longer the furnace would hold out, or when summer broke earlier than usual and we wanted to get out of the city for a weekend. But we would never clean anything we had made, it was all their stuff, cuff to collar, and when they left with it they hadn't taken anything of ours with them.

I missed the joy of making the quilts though and knew that Ezra did too. About a year after we stopped, we decided to make one more, and we decided that our last quilt would be the biggest and best one yet because we were making it for ourselves. Unlike the others, we didn't just start sewing, but sat down with some colored pencils and planned the whole thing out. It started as just a field with magnolia trees and crepe myrtle, but then Ezra drew in cotton and hoes, and finally all the slaves. In the corner was the river and freedom on the other side.

On the day that I was going to pick up the fabric, I looked at the picture again to make sure I got the colors right, and I saw that on the very top of the page, right on the other side of the water, Ezra had drawn in a woman's body with the wind blowing the magnolias so they fluttered over to meet her and it was just like I remembered it too.

That was the day I met Lily and a year before Percy Browne moved to the South Side for good.

By the time I met her, outside Colber's store, where I was going to buy cloth for what was supposed to be my last quilt, and she gave me a wink, she had just sold the baby and the hurt was still fresh. When I first saw her, I thought she was crazy like everyone else. Here she was wasting away to nothing in wet snow on cracked streets and winking at a stranger like we shared a secret. But Lily was sane. Her head was clear as a child's, it was just her love that had cracked.

After she lost Alice, there was nothing. She let herself go, tumbling to meet the nothingness head on.

Lily winked and I turned my head to see who was standing behind me. When I didn't see nobody, I gave her a nod, then turned away and rushed into the store.

"Who is that standing outside?" I asked Colber, as soon as the door was shut. He walked over to the window behind the counter and peeped out.

"I don't know," he said. "They call her Lily, said she sold her baby down by the pier for twenty dollars and a bottle of Scotch."

"She ain't colored, is she?" I asked, 'cause I hadn't looked at her good and it was hard to tell sometimes, especially here in the city.

"White as her name. Now what a white lady doing selling her child, I don't know. That's just what people say. Anything else I can help you with today, Miss Antoinette?"

When I gave him my order his eyebrows went up a little but he went to the back and came out with everything I had asked him for. "What you working on?" he asked while he added it all up.

"Me and Ezra making a quilt, something special."

"Must be special with all this fabric." He finished adding it up and gave me a little off before I handed over the money and he wrapped everything up with a string. When he finished, the package was so big that I could hardly see over the top of it.

"You need help with that, Miss Antoinette? I can have it delivered as soon as that boy gets here."

"No, Mr. Colber, I'll be fine. Thank you though." As I watched him wrap all of it, I saw in my mind exactly where each piece of fabric would go and was anxious to start working on it. I don't know what I would have done if I had to wait God knows how long to have it delivered.

"All right, I guess I'll see you next time then, but be careful on the way home, you know how quick the streets can ice over," Colber said, then came around and opened the door for me. I thanked him again before heading out.

He just wanted the extra money he charged for delivery. But I liked walking the six blocks back to my house. Even beneath the paper, I could feel each piece of cloth and thought about exactly which stitches I would use to hold them in place.

I should have known better. I should have woke Ezra up and had him come down with me, but I had wanted to get started while the excitement was still fresh. Half a block from Colber's, my shoe caught on the hem of a woman's coat and I tripped to the ground. Before I got up, I looked around me and saw a red-faced Lily still squatting against the building.

"Sorry about that," she said, letting go of her petticoat and rushing over to help me up. I don't know who I was more embarrassed for. "Are you okay?"

I wasn't wearing gloves and the skin on my right knuckle had pulled back. "I'm fine" was all I could say though. I gathered my boxes and started to go home. After a few steps, I turned back and saw Lily sitting back down in the snow, the bottom of her coat lying limp next to the rest of her.

"Miss," I called after her. When she turned and looked up at me, her eyes was puffy and wet. "You got somewhere to stay?"

She shook her head no.

"Well, why don't you come home with me and let me fix that coat for you."

"No, I'll be, I'll be fine," she said, trembling a l ittle. In the end I brought her back with me anyway and put on some coffee as I started to sew her hem back on.

When Ezra came in the kitchen and saw a white woman, who looked crazy as the moon, he doubled back for an instant before looking at me with a puzzled look. "Lily, this is my brother, Ezra," I said. Lily held her hand out and Ezra took it, then they both looked at me. "Ezra's deaf," I said. "He can't hear or talk." I never used the word dumb because it sounded so ugly and because Ezra was anything but dumb. He just couldn't talk.

Ezra went over to the packages and opened them, pulling out each piece of fabric one by one and stacking them on the table. I gave him a scornful look, because it didn't seem right, like eating in front of the hungry.

"That's lovely fabric," Lily said. "Who taught you to sew?"

"Just something I picked up from my mamma down south," I told her.

"Where down south?"

"Louisiana, where we're from."

"Oh, I sang in a club in New Orleans once, it was such a beautiful city. Why on earth did you leave?"

I started to say something, then Lily remembered where she was.

"I'm sorry. That was stupid of me."

"You don't have to apologize, Miss Lily. It's not your fault." There was an awkward silence as I finished sewing the coat and Lily started rambling about how she used to sing and how much her daddy and mamma hated it and said it would be the ruin of her.

"I guess they were right," she finally said, her eyes

looking at a piece of floor between me and the table. "Who ever would have guessed that I . . ." Then she trailed off.

"That you what?" I asked her.

"That I would end up like this," she said. She didn't feel sorry for herself though, she just hurt.

"Well, at least you got your health," I said. Then it was my turn to feel stupid. When folks hit the bottom and keep falling, the last thing they want is their health.

Lily started crying softly and I went around to her and put my hand on her back as Ezra got up to leave the room. "It's okay," I said. "Whatever it is, it'll be all right."

"Antoinette, I sold my daughter."

What do you say to that? She was a stranger. I kept rubbing her shoulders and let her cry. When the coffee was ready I poured her a cup with extra sugar and put it in front of her for when she would want it, then started making dinner. As the beans boiled Ezra came back into the room and started cutting out the pieces for the quilt. Lily drank her coffee and the winter night kept closing in.

After dinner, I drew her a hot bath in the old tub, then left the room so she could be alone. When she got out of her bath she looked like a different woman than the one who went in. I guess I hadn't realized how dirty she was before. Dirt or not, I made her a pallet on the living room floor, then went back to the kitchen to look over the quilt pieces.

A little while later, it might have been thirty minutes, the door pushed open and Lily came into the kitchen and leaned against the back of the door. "Thank you," she said. "I don't know—"

"No, Lily, it's just shelter. I can't give back what

you lost." She didn't say anything, but stood standing by the door for a while longer before saying goodnight, then going back to the living room.

That was a year ago and Lily had been singing some since then and even managed to keep her own apartment. In twelve months we had grown close as sisters, but no amount of love or shelter could replace what she had lost. She would always have that look of sadness wrapped around her, and no matter how good things got, the bottom would always stare her down sorrowfully when she was alone.

For a long time her answer had been to never be alone. The two of us spent all of our time together and when I had to run errands or do chores, she and Ezra would sit around making signs in the air until finally she taught him how to read and write and the notes they passed back and forth made as much sense as the language me and him shared.

Then they had a world that I was locked out of, even though I was happy Ezra had someone else he could talk to. It turned me into the one that was alone.

Maybe that's why I took to Percy so much at first, because he knew one of my memories and could talk about it louder than the voice in my own head.

People said that he had been living up in Canada for the last twenty years but the winters there was as cold as here and he said if he was going to die from the cold, then at least it would be one he knew.

He had knocked at my door just as I was cleaning the dishes from the table and thinking that I would make another quilt after all, just for myself. I stood up and moved to the door slowly when I heard the knock, afraid that it would be someone whose order I hadn't finished yet. When I opened the door though, I saw a stranger dressed to the nines and holding an armload of shirts.

"It'll be a week before I can even look at your order, Mister. You might want to take them somewhere else if you need them back before that," I said without inviting him in.

"No hurry, Miss. They been dirty for this long, another week won't hurt." He grinned. "Besides, people tell me you do the best work around."

"Okay, bring them in here and set them over on that table," I told him, holding the door open. "You must be new to town."

"Well, I used to live here, been away for a while though. You don't remember me, do you?"

Of course I didn't remember him. If I had I would have said so when I first saw him. "No. I don't think we've ever met. Your shirts will be ready next Wednesday," I said, putting an end to the conversation.

"Percy Browne. Sound familiar?"

"No. Wait." A spark went off in my head but it didn't catch. "No. I can't recall, I'm sorry." There was the shadow of a pause, and I hoped that I hadn't offended him into taking his business somewhere else, but that he would take himself in that direction.

"We met in Louisiana, must have been twenty years ago. I was the man that helped you and your little brother get out."

My eyes lit up. "Oh my God. I'm so sorry. I couldn't place you. What did you say your name was? Browne. Would you like to come in for a cup of coffee or some lunch, Mr. Browne?" He declined though, saying he had other business to tend to. I felt like a fool for not remembering him but couldn't really figure out whether I should have thrown my arms around him or closed the door on that part of my life.

When he left, I went back inside to tell Ezra just what had happened, then for the first time I could remember, I felt alone with my brother. There was no needlework for memories like that and I suddenly felt how incomplete my life with him really was. I had never had the past walk out of my memory and through my front door before. The shock was numbing and joyful at the same time and I wanted to talk about it, not just to anyone but to my brother, who had lived it too. There was no telling where Lily was and no one else to talk to about it except maybe Jeremiah, and I wouldn't see him again until Sunday.

I walked back to the front and got the shirts, started miming desperately to Ezra, acting out the whole awful night, whipping my arms like they were holding reins to show who I meant. Then I pointed to the shirts, but Ezra stared at me blankly. I threw the shirts in a ball on the table and went into my room and crumpled in a heap on the bed.

After a while I got up and opened the trunk where we kept the quilt we had made for Mamma. I went back to the kitchen and took a stretch of the new material and ripped a piece off, then cut out shapes for me and Ezra and a carriage and a carriage man and put them next to Mamma by the river. I held them tacked there with my fingers and shook them in front of Ezra's face. When I got the same blank stare, I started screaming at him but he just held my arms still and shook his head. He didn't remember the man.

I wanted to rip the quilt in half. He probably didn't remember Mamma either, just the sight of a dead body by some water or maybe not even that and he thought the quilt was just making pictures with fabric. He was so young.

I took the quilt and put it back in the truck, got a jacket, and went out for some air. When I turned the corner, at the end of our block I saw Jeremiah walking toward me from the other direction. I took a few more steps, then crossed the street. I don't know what took hold of me but I couldn't stand to see him, knew I wouldn't be able to stand the small talk and awkwardness. I doubled back before he could recognize me and took the alleyway back to the house.

I don't know how long I was gone; it couldn't have been more than fifteen minutes, but when I opened the door I could hear Lily and Ezra in the front room. Not just sounds, but voices, two of them. Lily's I knew right away, but the other voice was low and gravelly, like it had been pulled up from the throat of a dead person.

I couldn't go into that room. I pounded my fists on the kitchen tabletop. No, goddamnit. I felt like I had been kicked in the stomach. Not because the two of them was together; I had known that for months and didn't care. I felt like I had been betrayed deeper than flesh.

Lily walked in and touched her hand to my shoulder and asked what was wrong until I lifted my head and sobbed, "He was talking. Ezra was talking to you."

"Toni, he wasn't talking, I swear. They were just sounds. I was as shocked as anyone the first time, but I swear they're just sounds."

"But I heard him. It sounded like—"

"I know, Toni. I'm sorry you had to hear. . . ."

Lily turned a deep red. I guess she was so startled she had forgot to be embarrassed. And I felt wicked for having heard the two of them. I wiped my eyes with the sleeve of my jacket, then stood up. "No, I'm the one who should be sorry, Lily. I don't know what's wrong with me today, but seeing him at my door just set something off." I told Lily what had happened, about Mr. Browne showing up out of nowhere, about not being able to talk, and about running away from Jeremiah. She just sat there listening until I had finished, and by then Ezra had come out in the kitchen too.

Lily wrote something down on a piece of paper, and Ezra walked over and gave me a hug. Then he wrote something on the other side of the paper. "He says he's sorry he can't remember," Lily read out. Then I told her to tell him it wasn't his fault. We went back and forth like that for God knows how long, with Lily sitting between us translating, and me and Ezra smiling for all we were worth.

I skipped church the next day and Lily started teaching me letters. Nothing much, first she taught me how to make all the letters of the alphabet, holding my hand steady whenever I made a wrong move. Then she taught me how to write my name. When I finally got all the letters lined up right, I couldn't stop staring at it: "A-n-t-o-i-n-e-t-t-e." It looked strange seeing a bunch of lines that was supposed to be me. After she had left, I kept staring at it with pride, even when I took out my fabric and started working on the new quilt.

I didn't start out with a design. I just sat down with the intention of making a quilt for the two of them. I used some material I had left over and let the colors pick themselves. I was too absorbed to care much when I pricked my fingers; I just pressed the tips until the bleeding stopped.

I worked on the quilt until I fell asleep, and when I woke up the next morning I started sewing again without bothering to eat. I kept it up I don't know how long until I realized that I was trying to quilt memory and didn't have any idea what it should look like. In the day I sewed and at night it seemed like I went back and undid everything I had made. I kept it up for four days until I found the right patterns.

There was a knock at the door and as soon as I heard it I remembered that I hadn't even looked at Mr. Browne's shirts since he dropped them off. I opened the door and let him in, then quickly apologized to him. I could have them by tomorrow.

"Don't worry about the shirts. Are you all right? You look feverish?"

"I'm fine," I told him, and would he like a cup of tea? Seeing him didn't startle me this time, just the opposite: I hadn't realized until then that I had been waiting for him to come back.

He sat down on the couch and I went to the kitchen to put some water on. When I came back, he was standing at the window looking out on the street. "Sure is good to be back here," he said. He went on about Canada and talked some about the Railroad and told me how he was born in Mississippi, and the whole time I just stared at him until his words started to break apart and he stopped talking.

I saw him again the next day and the one after that and the fourth time is when he knelt down on my living room floor and held my hand, asking me to be his wife. I should have said no. The least I could have done would have been to wait until I knew what kind of man he really was and not just his shirt size. I didn't think though, I said yes and threw my arms around him.

Later that night, when I told Ezra and Lily, they looked at me strange, then they both hugged me.

Lily went on about how a woman should always

marry a man older than her, and not make the mistake she had with a younger one, and then she started in right away on the plans. Where it would be held, where we would live afterward. I hadn't given them that much thought—I guess I hadn't really thought that it would change things so, but there was a lot I hadn't thought about.

THANK GOD THE children were born healthy. Lily said you could tell by their eyes; both of theirs clear as a summer morning. We waited for days, every morning checking their eyes before feeding or diaper changing, but they never came down with it.

She started telling me what it did, but she softened it in the telling, maybe not, but nothing prepared me for it. When I first told her what was happening, she knew right away and went and got me all kinds of salts and balms and such, and they helped the pain, but a few weeks later I woke up with the fever, and it never left.

In the end I heard voices. Mamma and Ezra and Lily and Percy and Miss Harris and the twins crying all at the same time. They circled around my bed and weighted on me like a press and I couldn't tell them apart and I couldn't tell the voices from the faces or the colors from the light. And the voices stopped and the wild dreams started and I was standing in a field back down south right where I started and a voice told me to follow it and I chased the voice through the fields to a hill that just got steeper and steeper, past the preacherman, past Percy, past Ezra and Lily and Alice and the twins and a door opened. Then an angel came and gave me a chair because I had come so far and was so tired and the pain fell and the colors rose. Rose up around me clear as a memory to circle around me and the lights fell and the pain rose and the voices fell, and the door closed, tight.

Tight as the shroud of memory.

Once, I did not know the difference
between Niger and Nigger.

Now, with my lover, I pronounce
Ni-ger.
This is a river.
Nig-ger.
These are people.

Nigger
I am three hundred years old,
half-caste, and born on the middle passage.

Niger
I am the water. The unknowable.

Women as black as jet
men dark as pitch.
Under African skies.

And Mississippi moons
After we crossed the big river
on a bridge made of wood and paper.

Now I recross on a road
of human backs, resurrected
expressly for the purpose
of bringing me home.

Before I go I must visit my father
in the attic where he paints.
"Here," he says, holding my fingers to the canvas.
"This is the river."

I touch it and remember
to tell him that he is beautiful.

Then I go to my mother's garden.
I place my hands in the soil beside her.
It is black and warm.
This is where they made the New World.

"Take these with you,
so that you do not go hungry," she tells me.

In that same soil
I laid with my lover
Sometimes, placing my hands
on her pains.
Other times, I parted her thighs
to linger in moistness there.

Before I go I must stop
in Antigua and Cuba
to pick up pots of curried goat from my uncles

and Aruba for a certain root
which can make a good medicine
when mixed with cassava.

"Do not go home empty-handed.
Take these with you and tell everyone
that we think of them."

"It is too bad that our brothers
could not come for the party,
it is such a long journey."

Has my love gone bitter?
Is my lover still alive?

I must remember my boots
the ones for rain.
I must remember my keys
the ones for chains.

When I am safe and dry
in my mother's house
with warm, dry feet,
she holds me in the light.

"Let me look at you, my, how you have grown."

Many things have happened
since I left
(colonialism, neocolonialism,
two-revolutions,
three-coups, and more neocolonialists).

In my father's garden
my cousins surround me with the truth.

*"You look different, there are scars
on your skin. Your tongue is twisted.
Your home has burned down."*

*I lay with my lover.
She feels heavy in my arms
and smooth to my tongue.*

*"Tomorrow we must sacrifice to the gods
for bringing you home.
We must build a house."*

*We make love
face up
face down.*

*The earth, the wind,
the sky, my people. Ase. Ase.
I do not forget that I love her.*

*In the morning
we will prepare a ram. It is a big sacrifice
but I have been gone a long time,*

*long enough to create
a revolution, two-histories
(a short one and a long one)*

and the New World.

*In the morning, in the Old World
we offer libations
of palm wine.*

The earth, the wind,
the sky, my people
Ase. Ase.

When finally I remember
how the ceremony goes
I take the calabash to pour a bit more.

The longest drink of the palm wine
for my lover
my lover who is not here.

Richard

The soft belly of Africa poked through the clouds, nappy lights dotted the ground, and a whole continent full of nothing but black folks reached up with a raised fist. I raised mine back.

I thought I had left the last of the ofays back in America. But before the seat belt light went out, this crazy cracker leaned against me and asked what tribe I was from and could he take a picture.

"From the tribe of your mama, asshole."

I pushed past him and got my bag from the overhead. Nothing in it except a few pair of blue jeans, some shorts, a sleeping bag, and Sly's beat-up army boots that he gave to me when he got back from his first tour in Nam. The second one didn't go so well.

He had no business over there in the first place. I had better sense. Wasn't about to get my ass blown off fighting for no piece of mud in a swamp that didn't mean shit to me no way. Besides, bullshit government just sending us out like buffalo soldiers.

Saved my little scratch and got me the first bird I could. Black man's country.

I left the airport and got a cab. On the way, I asked the driver where the action was and he took me to this jive-ass joint with nothing but a bed in the room and the shower all the way at the end of the hall that I had to share with half a dozen people. By the time he dropped me off it was already dark and I didn't want to be wandering around at night until I got my bearings.

I put my bag under the bed and washed my face, then went down to the bar across the street. The outside was a broken-down building, and even bathed in the dim drinking light, the inside was just as filthy.

I tried to start up a conversation with the bartender, old cat, had a million years of Mama Africa carved in his face. His English was choppy though. He just kept smiling and nodding his head. Sad, man—black people can't even talk to each other 'cause they fucked up our heads so much. I finished my drink and went back to the hotel.

There was nobody around except a couple of German tourists, so I went up to my room and tried to catch some sleep. The minute I turned out the lights though, I could hear the rats and roaches and God knows what else scurrying across the floor and buzzing around the bed. I turned the lights back on and sat on the edge of the bed, looking out the window. Nothing but Africa as far as I could see. Tomorrow I would get out and start figuring the place out, but the first night I sat in my room excited and scared as hell.

The blood inside of me was running hot and I sat

keeping vigil and listening to the night noises of the city. Not just usual city sounds but Nairobi night noises punching through my other thoughts while the rest of the city slept.

By the time the first warmth touched the ground, the hum of a few beat-up cars cut through the air, familiar, lulling me like a gospel. Finally, I fell asleep.

I woke up around noon, to the sound of my stomach grumbling, and realized that I hadn't eaten since before my flight. I walked to the end of the hall, opened the bathroom door, thought better of it, and went out to find something to eat. There was nothing around except some dirty-looking shacks with dirty people in them, cooking I don't know what. But I hadn't eaten since my flight, so I went into the cleanest-looking one.

I guess I expected to find some okra and collard greens. But when I saw the shit they were serving, my stomach turned and I resigned myself to not eating. Instead, I ordered some tea, reluctantly used the sugar they had left out on the table, and stared out onto the street.

After a while this cool-looking cat came over and sat next to me and asked if I wanted to dig a little reefer. He seemed enough down, so I finished the tea and followed him to a little shack around the corner.

The corrugated metal resting on top of clapboard and dirty kids running around were blowing my high, but the newness of everything was enough to keep me turned on. Every so often he would point at something in the room and teach me the Swahili word for it. Then he turned on this little radio and blew my mind. Here I was sitting in a shanty in the middle of Africa and James Brown starts singing and covering the whole room with soul.

We just sat there grooving, for what seemed like hours, until he asked me for some money. Then he tells me he got girls. All kinds. I told him I didn't fuck around with whores. Never paid for it in my life.

I left and eventually found a bus headed for the other side of town. The bodies inside were packed tight as a living wall, and the top was covered with squawking chickens. After a few stops my skin started crawling so much that I had to get off. I had lost my high and didn't know exactly where I was. I went into a little bar with reggae blaring from a tiny outside speaker, hanging from a wire like the rest of the country, to ask for directions.

The minute I stepped in, everybody stopped what they were doing and started staring at me like they had never seen a black person before. I sat down at the end of the bar and ordered a drink. The beer was served warm in a dusty little bottle that looked like they didn't throw them away after you finished, just refilled it and passed it on, germs and all, to the next sucker.

After a while, the boldest drunk came over and sat next to me.

"Welcome home, brother," he said, throwing a limp arm around my shoulder.

"Yeah, well, it's good to be here," I lied.

We talked for a while and all the other cats stared at us while he kept telling me that we was both black people, one skin and all that shit. I might have believed him a week ago, but I wasn't standing there next to him. After a while, I had had enough adventure for the day and grew tired of him. When he figured out that I wasn't up for talking or being taken, he got up and wobbled back over to play cards with his friends.

I left to find a new hotel, something with a real shower. There was no way I was sleeping in that ghetto again tonight.

I wandered around until I found a decent place that I could afford. At the bar I ran into a few brothers from home, army cats lucky enough to be stationed at the embassy. The first thing they asked me was if I was dodging the draft. If you were young and out of the country, you were either a cripple, a communist, or a coward. I was some of all of those things, but none of them really, and just enough of a cripple to keep my mother from losing another son.

"Naw, man, I got this bum leg, couldn't serve." They looked back at me like I was lying. "Shit, man, it ain't like if I saw Simon Legree walking around today, I wouldn't bust a cap in his ass."

Sly signed up just to make the old man happy, follow in his footsteps and all that patriarchy shit. The old man and his twin brother was both in the second war and you think he would have better sense than to send his son.

I really did have a bad leg. Fucked it up playing ball with this hack. Jump shot. Easy. He went up with me. Had no hop though, so he pushed all that chitlin-eating fat against my legs. I came down wrong. If he hadn't shattered damn near all the bones in my left one, I would have put my good leg up his ass.

I guess they were satisfied enough with my story and I was lonely enough to go out with them that night.

We went to a nightclub outside the business district, nothing but a hole in the wall, and a block-long line of people waiting to get in. We walked right up to the front of the line, they knew the bouncer or something, and everybody behind us started grumbling and asking if we thought we was special. People could always tell if you didn't come from there.

As soon as we opened the door, the heat and hustle of the place grabbed us, pulled us up the narrow flight of stairs and out onto the dance floor. It wasn't like the movies. No drums and pygmies doing the Watusi, which might have been a little interesting, just a dinky nightclub filled with poseurs. Everybody in there was dressed to kill and the music was exactly what I would have heard at a friend's party or nightclub at home.

We got a few drinks and started peeping the action in all its dashiki and Afro glory. I was about to leave when my eyes fell on this fox wearing the shortest mini I'd ever seen. Hips and curves throbbing against my pupils while disco light beat against her naked shoulders. After a while she got tired of dancing and came over to the bar. I guess she had been checking me out too, at least I like to think so.

I bought her a drink and we talked for a while, then went out on the dance floor to shake those other cats loose. We did our thing for a while and I felt the heady rush you feel when everything is right and you're all but certain that you're about to get some. Then this big baboon-looking motherfucker steps up, you know, like "I'm king of this here jungle." He just stood there staring us down until I thought I was going to have to hand him some before she leaned in and told me he was her chaperon. Ain't that some shit.

He gave me his meanest look while she wrote her address down and told me to come by the house tomorrow.

I went back to the bar and those other fools were sitting there laughing their asses off. "You can't get none of that, man," one of them said.

I ignored him and watched her back while she walked out of the club, waiting to see if she would turn around. The baboon dude had a tight grip on her and she never looked back. I crumpled the address in my pocket, clutching it tight. Just making sure I didn't lose it.

I danced a while longer, just to show those dudes that I wasn't fazed, until my leg started to hurt and the first light of day was starting to break.

I woke up the next day with my head and leg throbbing all beat up, like I had played one-on-one with Wilt Chamberlain or somebody. I went to the hotel restaurant and bought lunch, then wandered around the city for a while until I mustered the courage to hail a cab and give the driver her address.

Nice crib, man, I never would have thought they had places like that in Africa. Big metal gate to keep the lions and shit out. I wished I had put on some nicer threads, but it was too late for wishing. I ambled up the steps and rang the doorbell.

A woman in a French-maid get-up came to the door and I told her I was there to see Imani. She closed the door in my face and went back inside. When it opened again there was this fat cat standing there who could only be her father.

"Who are you?"

"Umm, Richard. Richard Browne. Junior, sir," I threw in for good measure. Might as well pull out all the stops.

"What do you want, Mr. Richard Browne, Junior?"

"I came by to see Imani."

"Where are you from?"

"America."

"Well, we do things differently here, Richard. You do not come to my door and ask to see my daughter, it is improper."

"Who should I ask to see, sir?"

"You ask for permission to see her."

I wished I had brought some flowers for the old lady, something to butter these cats up with.

"Well, sir, with your permission, I would like to visit with your daughter Imani."

He checked me out, looking extra hard at my boots, like he was trying to tell me I was way out of my league, but he opened the door.

He led me down this long hall and into a sitting room. I waited until his fat ass was almost on the sofa before I started to lower myself. Old cats dig that shit. As soon as I had crossed my legs, he started working me. He was like a grand inquisitor, asking about my family and what I'm doing in Africa and what I'm doing with my life and all that shit. I guess he was pretty satisfied though, because after about ten minutes of that shit, Imani walked in the room, and he got up and walked out.

I was surprised that he left us alone. He must have been kind of impressed when I kicked it to him about the old man and all that shit. Evil motherfucker was good for something after all.

To tell the truth, I was scared my knees would start knocking when I stood up. I was trying hard to hold it together. I'd only been in the country three days and I was already about to fuck the president's daughter or whatever the hell he did to get a house that bad in a country that tore down.

She sat there all prim and proper and we just shot the shit. Same-old same-old. It was a hard place to talk, what with her old man and God knows who else lurking around the corner waiting to see if I tried to touch her or something. But it was still cool. I knew that if I could get her out of this fucking mausoleum we could talk.

"Why don't we go out and grab something to eat?" I just threw it out, not really expecting anything to happen. But she said okay, then went into the other room and came back with a jacket.

"I have to be back by three," she warned me as I helped her put her jacket on.

We were almost at the door when her pops came back. He just stood there in the doorway and gave me this hard-ass look. Then he tried his best to fake a smile but you could tell he was just faking, the corners started falling too soon. I met him head-on though.

"It was a pleasure meeting you, sir, I hope we can talk again."

"Have her back by three o'clock," he said. Then he shook my hand, pressing it a little too firmly, like he was about to cut my throat with the other one.

We went to this little joint that served Italian food. First decent meal I had since I got there. The maître'd gave her a little nod while we was waiting for our table.

"Who is your father anyway?" I asked her.

"He's the editor of the *Gazette*." That explained some shit. Like how he knew who my father was and why we was getting all this first-class treatment.

"Don't mind him. He's all bark. I'm the only daughter," she said as this dude in a white and gold-trimmed monkey suit led us to our table.

We sat down and talked some more about the usual shit. Same questions her father asked, but sweeter, you know, like she really gave a damn.

Under the table our legs kept knocking against each other and we smiled all nervous. She had the damndest smile, man. I swear those teeth made me want to cry. Just teeth, but set perfect in her face like Michelangelo or somebody had put them there. Rest of her was like that too.

I reached across the table and took her hand. Just to hold it.

"Are you the only child?" she asked me, to take some of the edge off all the electricity flying through the room.

"Naw, I'm in the middle. I got an older brother, Kurt, and a younger brother, Sly. Sly is just a year younger than me. Was, I should say. He died 'cause my old man decided he needed somebody to join the army, Kurt was already married and in graduate school, and I couldn't serve. Sly went out like a man though. Even though I think Nam is all fucked up, I know my little brother was a hell of a soldier. Only nineteen when they iced him."

"Iced? What is that?"

Her English was pretty good for an African. Even though it was the official language of the country, almost everybody spoke it all fucked up. But hers was pretty good. Still, she had problems understanding sometimes.

I broke it down for her, then told her all about how Pops was a lieutenant in World War II. They just made him an officer 'cause he was a lawyer, but still he led a little squad of brothers into battle once and he was making damn sure nobody was going to forget that. After the war he started a practice with his twin brother, Uncle Sherman, and later got some appointment or other from the government. People always kissing his ass 'cause they didn't know what a bastard he was. Sly, Sylvester, joined up 'cause I

84

couldn't go. Fucked his head all up. When he came home, me and Moms was psyched that he made it out of there, but Pops just beamed and told him how he would make officer in no time and how the army is a fine place for colored men to prove themselves and all kinds of shit.

Sly never could stand up to that bastard and I hated both of them for it. Here was a real war going on all around us and Sly listened to the old man tell him how he was a service to his country and people. Shit, he was halfway around the world, what the fuck good was that doing his people? Sly bought the shit though. I think he really believed it deep down, and went back for another tour.

They said one of his own men shot him, a brother at that. It wasn't the official version. Those bastards in Washington never tell you what happened. Pops knew some people though. Turned out Sly decided one day that he was tired of fighting. He just walked away from his squad. Went into the jungle ranting about how his mind was falling apart. They said he was talking all kinds of crazy shit, but mostly he just kept saying how he couldn't fight no more. Sly walked away. I'm proud of him for that. At first they thought it was just a spell, I guess that kind of shit happened all the time over there. But after a while, when he didn't come back, they sent a squad out to search for him. I don't really know what happened after that, all the stories took different turns there, but the point was he wasn't going to fight no more goddamned war.

The most believable version was that one of the dudes in the search squad got all freaked out, maybe 'cause Sly said something that got to him, but before anybody could stop it, he fired a couple of rounds, then slit Sly's throat with his bayonet. They said Sly didn't even try to stop it. He just laid against the tree he had picked out and took it. He knew what time it was. People know shit like that.

When we finished eating, it was almost three o'clock and I didn't want to piss her old man off, so we got a cab and I escorted her home. It was a trip, like an old movie where the dude is supposed to be some kind of gentleman.

I did slip my fingers between hers, lacelike, and when we got to her crib, I gave her a little kiss. Not a big one, just enough to know. It was enough to know. Bells and whistles and shit going off in my head. You know how it is when you kiss somebody and your mouth lines up just right with hers.

I wasn't sprung or nothing, just kind of lonely, and like I said, she was cool. Besides, I still had to take care of business, you know, go and finish college and all that shit. It's not like I was thinking of living there or nothing, but it just seemed like whenever good shit happens, it's the wrong place, wrong time, wrong number.

It's not like I'd never been in love, but that was back when I was just a kid and nothing meant what you thought it meant. The first time you get a little, you're always guaranteed to pretty much think you're in love, just 'cause you're getting some. You think it's supposed to be like that every time. It takes a while before you realize that it doesn't happen like that all the time, so when you find something that feels real, you hold it tight.

It felt real enough with Imani, so I held on tight, even though there were a few things about her that I didn't especially like. For one thing, she was study- ing British literature at the university, as if black people never wrote nothing up. Still, I guess it can't

hurt to know that kind of shit, at least you got something to talk about at cocktail parties. There was
some other stuff too, but it was all pretty petty. Like
I said, it felt real.

It was the end of summer and her school was
starting back up, which made it easier to see her
'cause she lived in a dorm with these other chicks
and they were all masters at sneaking dudes in and
each other out.

Being around campus put an incredible pressure
on me to get my own life together though. I had had
what the doctors called a breakdown right before I
dropped out. It was really just all those white cats
getting on my nerves and I just felt like I needed to
connect. With anything. I left with only three se-
mesters to go before graduation and coming here
was supposed to help me get my mind together. But
I had already been here nearly two months and I
knew I probably wouldn't be any less fucked up
when I got back. But the gnawing sense of isolation
I had felt on campus was ebbing.

Before I dropped out, I had stayed in my room for
six weeks without leaving and without speaking to
anyone. Finally, the dean called my parents and they
came and took me home. After hanging around the
house for a couple of months, I told them I wanted
to spend a few months in Africa and promised that
when I came back I would finish up school. I just
needed a break from people.

But in the month and a half that I had been with
Imani, we had spent all of our time together and
somehow she managed a balance between going out
all the time with me and finishing her studies. I remember a week at the ocean together, smoking
joints and laying up in bed whenever we weren't in

the water. You should have seen her on the beach, a blue striped bathing suit on her curves and a white knapsack on her back. Out of sight, man.

It was the best week I ever had. She was on a mid-semester break and told her parents she was going out to Mombasa with some girlfriends. Instead, we rented a cottage on Lamu and spent the whole week making love. We would wake up in the morning and these cats would come around with fresh fruit—coconuts and shit. About five minutes later, here's another cat with all this fish, first catch of the day. We would cook it up and smoke a little, then head out to the water.

Bluest water I've ever seen, and they had these little boats you could rent to go snorkeling. Nothing more than a couple of logs thrown together any kind of way, like something you would make in the basement, but they did the trick. We'd go half a mile out to the reef and drop the makeshift anchor, then spend the rest of the morning swimming through schools of fish and chasing each other around the boat.

After that we would go back to the little cottage and hang around talking about all kinds of shit, anything that came to our heads. She would tell me something about Africa and I would tell her something about America, joking every now and then about how cool our kids would turn out. She never leaned on me about shit, we just hung out and everything was always right. I know it doesn't sound like too much special but I guess it was the way we vibed more than anything else.

Me and her old man even started getting along after that. He usually just asked me questions about my pops. Like did he really call so-and-so a son of a bitch to his face, shit like that. It was still hard for him to imagine a black man telling a white dude off. He stopped tripping so much about what I was going to do with my life after I started telling him how interested I was in business. It was just some bullshit I told him to keep him from asking all those goddamned questions about what I was doing with my life and shit.

But we all knew that I was leaving pretty soon and I don't think they were ever too happy about how serious we seemed about each other. He never knew how deep it went, but he saw enough to know that one of us couldn't help but get hurt. I tried not to think about shit like that too much though and just enjoy it.

At night we would go out and do quiet shit, the theater and all that. Didn't have to worry about bumping into nobody else. Every now and then we would go to a club and show them motherfuckers how to get down. My arms around her, her arms around me, and no thoughts about anything else. Until about a month after we got back from the coast, one night when we had decided to stay in, and were hanging out in my room.

The people I was boarding with were going out and we would have the house to ourselves. I had moved out of the hotel about a week before we left for the coast and rented a little room with this family. They were Kikuyu and had a son my age who was at school in England so they enjoyed the idea of having me around to fill the empty space. When they went out to the country to visit relatives, they piled me in the backseat and carried me along and watched with amusement as I tried to milk a cow or some other farm chore. It was cool enough, but the farm was a shabby piece of dirt that never yielded much. I think they helped the relatives out with money, just enough so they didn't lose the place and to keep them from all moving to the city and into the living room.

They never got on my ass about shit though and let me come and go as I pleased. *"mtoto wa* America." American son. I think they especially liked it that I was going out with a local girl and not chasing after expatriates and whatnot.

Anyway, Imani was sitting on the edge of the bed, dangling one foot, and I was all stretched out across it. I was teasing her, joking around like you do with your woman, talking about this and that. And she just blurted it out without warning, and I sat there stunned.

I couldn't imagine myself walking around trying to be somebody's father. I mean, part of me was saying, Yeah, baby, beautiful. Beautiful. And I wanted to pull her close and hold on tight as skin. I wanted to. But something stopped me. The other part. Part that says, "Pull out. Pull out no matter how warm she feels around you. Pull out. Spill the seed." The voice I should have listened to a month ago.

The kid would probably come out all fucked up anyway. I don't think I had any problems with her being African or anything, motherland Mama. I had too much other shit I needed to take care of when I got back. I just couldn't stay here. Too young, too far from home. Too fucked up myself.

"Listen, baby. I love you but . . . ain't it somebody you can go to? You know." Yeah, she knew.

She broke down and started crying. What was I supposed to do? I had my arm around her but I couldn't manage anything else from my mouth. She started flipping out all hysterical, saying she was going to have her father call mine and a bunch of other crazy shit.

Mrs. Morurie knocked on the door as she was leaving. "Everything okay in there?"

"Yes, ma'am, everything's all right." My life is just fucked up is all. "We're just talking." Fuck man, I couldn't even begin to think about spending the rest of my life in Africa or taking her back home.

"Come on, sugar, don't start with that. Of course I mean it when I say I love you." We probably never would have met if I hadn't been so lonely. I can say that now, no shame in being lonely. I don't know, maybe that's how everything starts. Two people just find each other when they're lonely in the same way.

"Yeah, baby. I love you."

Finally, I got her to agree to it. I told her I would give her the money and everything—whatever it took. But she didn't want me to go with her. Woman's business, she called it. You know how it is. I told her I was coming anyway though. I figured the least I could do was go with her.

A week later, we drove out to the bush. Baked-mud buildings topped by thatched roofs and set against a backdrop of cornfields and dense red mountains. Naked kids and flies buzzing around everywhere, chicks carrying pots around on their heads.

We went up to one of the huts and she starts rapping to this old lady too fast for me to keep up. The old lady just shot me this nasty-ass look and they went into the hut. There was nothing for me to do except hang around outside, smoking cigarettes and sorry I ever agreed to come in the first place. I should have just let her take care of it like she wanted to.

All these kids start swarming around, asking for money and where was I from. I gave them a couple of coins. They looked so goddamn pathetic, man. Then I noticed all these dudes hanging out at another hut and walked over to check out what they was doing.

They were sitting in a circle in the shade getting pretty loose and passed me this bucket full of something that smelled like yeast. I kind of put it up to my lips, playacting like I was drinking the shit.

One of them saw what was going on and started yelling at me, asking if I thought I was too good to share a drink with them, just tripping. I couldn't do anything but take a sip of the shit. I was only a little surprised when I didn't throw up but I took another sip anyway and sat down in their circle.

"No rain," one of them told me. The land was barren, I saw looking out at the hills ringing the village. It was harsh and beautiful country and for exactly one instant I felt connected to it. Fifty feet away the woman I thought I loved lay in a hut with my child. She might just as easily be giving birth to it.

If she was it would have been a stillbirth.

I was happy as hell when one of the kids ran over and pointed at Imani, standing next to the car waiting. It was finally over.

I walked over to her and gave her a little kiss. She sort of turned her head as we got in the car. Going back to the city, she didn't say much, just sat there singing to herself. Wouldn't talk about how it went or nothing. I figured she was just shook up. She did ask me what I was talking to those old cats about. Not too much. Then she starts going off, saying she could see the disgust on my face when I was talking to them. Fuck it. I couldn't argue with her. You can never argue with a woman who has seen what she has seen or remembers what she remembers.

We didn't spend as much time together after that. She was busy with school every time I tried to go see her. I just did my own thing, and stopped even trying to see her. It hurt me though whenever I thought about it. Everywhere I went was something that meant something to us. I couldn't stop thinking of how it might have been if it had been different and knew that it was time to leave.

She drove me to the airport, but it was all pretty awkward. By then I just wanted to get the fuck out of there. Too much hurt. Motherfucking airplane was nearly three hours late. Nothing works right in Africa.

The departing flight finally landed and I gave Imani a little hug and she squeezed me real tight, I guess to show that everything we went through was real and really meant something to her too. After we stopped hugging, she held my hands and just stared at me. I was hoping she wouldn't cry, that was the last thing I needed. *Just don't cry.*

She pulled me toward her and held my hands on her stomach, then gave a little squeeze. We kissed for the last time and I walked down the corridor to get the plane. As soon as I got in my seat, I started thinking about the first meal I would have when I got back. What I would do about school. Anything. I even started talking to this white dude from Texas sitting next to me. It turned out he went to the same college a few years back. He had been living in Africa a few years and we spent a couple of hours talking about all the crazy shit that happens in Africa. Mama Africa.

They turned off the lights and soon everybody on the plane fell asleep. I stared out the window, watching the sky outside getting bigger and bigger, until all you could see below was the mound of the coast where it met the water. And the only thing I could think of as I sat there was how my bed smelled when Imani rolled over in the morning. Like fresh-cut flowers.

$\mathbf{F}$or years I wandered help-
lessly in the loneliest stretches of the desert in search
of the tree. Foolishly, I labored to tell the differences
between one reach of sand and another.

In the mornings I awoke sweating in the grip of
the sun's fingers. I lumbered to my feet and walked
deeper into the desert, moving forward only by rote.
As the days passed, I covered less and less distance,
moving slowly to my death.

On a miserable day as the sun finally began to go
down, I reached a set of footprints. This is how I
would reach my end. The man who walked in a circle through the world until he found himself back
at the womb, having learned nothing. I fell to the
ground, resigning myself to the spot of my grave. But
as I looked to the sky, I saw a man whose face was
the face of the desert and whose eyes filled me with
the fear of time. My eyes met his and he spoke to

me. "I have watched your journey," he said. "I have seen the circle of your sad life."

He beckoned to me and I followed him, keeping a few paces behind as I tried to figure out where I would run to if I needed to run. But after walking only a short distance I saw it.

The tree of my childhood stories grew before me in the distance. It was beautiful and I began to run toward it, my body filled with joy. I began to cry and to scream, and finally, as I reached the shadow of the tree, I began to pray.

But in the light of the tree I saw that its branches were immense, its height unmeasurable. How did I think that I would ever be able to take from it? Fool. Even with thirty men beneath me, I would not be able to reach the lowest of it's branches. A man who knows things would wait under the tree for it to offer its gift. I understood now why my grandfather had never left home. Not because he was afraid, but because he was brave. He was waiting. If I had grown up in the land that is mine, I would know things and perhaps my grandfather would have taught me to wait.

I was only a boy when I left and in my lifetime the tree might have bent down to me. But I had ravaged myself until I no longer knew why I had sought it out in the first place. The tree could not tell me who I was.

The old man stood beside me with sad eyes and I could tell that it was hard for him to look at my spent body, but he caressed my shoulders and led me toward the village gate.

When we reached my grandfather's hut, my guide led me through the small door, then departed. My grandfather cut a chunk of bread from his loaf and placed it in my mouth. Then he moved my body, which had grown as old as his own, from the hut into the shade of this tree.

"History," he said, "is an onion. But if you could ever pull back the skins, what you would see at the core is two fists, each holding half a heart. Husk the half hearts of history and you see a pile of gold bullion. In a witch's cauldron, bring the bullion to a slow boil. When the gold is melted you should find that it isn't pure, but contains two sheaves. Place the sheaves side by side on a clean and dry surface and you will find the name of an unborn child.

"Although you will forget this lifetime and many others before you learn." He paused. "Before you learn the secret of remembering, you will always hear this." And as I died in the shade of the tree, he leaned down and whispered the name into my ear.

Brenndan

Listen. The city is full of people like Brenndan. No one ever notices. Would it matter if he had been living alone on the streets since he was twelve, his body withered from lack of human touch? Or if he had been shipped off to boarding schools in Vermont and Switzerland and had learned about isolation that way? No. It does not matter which road he started on. He is here now and people look through him just the same. The world promised him everything. It delivered nothing.

He sat heavy-lidded in his cell rehearsing his death. It was a scene that he had gone over every day for as long as I had known him. The details had changed gradually over time, each year becoming increasingly lucid. Electric chair replaced firing squad in his imagination. Nameless executioner replaced enemy captains and paratroopers. Toy soldiers became living police.

A predisposition for risk had taught him to live with death, to become addicted to it. Years of hard drugs and petty crime had reinforced his addiction until he circled around his fate like a pilgrim making turns about the Kaaba.

By the time my brother arrived here he knew his death better than he had ever known how to live.

The first time I visited him in jail, his trial was nearly over and he made it perfectly clear that he had no intention of hanging around. Nothing left to do here. And had decided that he needed to die a long time ago, so why was it taking everyone on that goddamned jury so long to figure it out?

Looking at me, his eyes hung motionless in the air, his attention somewhere in the middle distance.

"I bet you dig seeing me here," he said. "You finally get to be on top."

"Naw, man. It's not like that. It's not like that at all." I reached my hand out toward him in a gesture of communion. He accepted it only with five limp fingers and an overgrown fingernail.

"You know I didn't do it." He pleaded for support.

"I know, Brenndan. We'll get you out of here," I said, reciting the necessary lie.

"I might of did it. I mean, it could have been me. It don't matter. Fuck it. Fuck all this."

"Brenndan, you didn't do it. We'll prove that." I could tell that he was high. The half-finished thoughts and the wandering eyes had grown familiar by now. I had already grown too far removed for B to ever confess his addiction to me, but the aging men I passed on street corners had taught me what bliss and bottom looked like when they were mingled. When I learned that Brenndan was a junkie I began to pay closer attention to those people.

They would be there, sure as the cement, laughing, shooting craps, and shooting the shit as sure as the Hawk in winter. My eyes linger on them for too long. They feel this stare and the hair on the back of their necks stands up. They turn and scowl at me. And I walk away satisfied because none of them is my brother.

Now as I looked at him, his head lolled back and his eyes drifted slowly into a junkie's nod. I watched him sleep and wondered if I would have recognized if one of those people had been him.

"Wake up. Wake up, damnit," a voice from another cell boomed out. "I can tell you're sleeping in there. Wake up, motherfucker. You ain't got no right to sleep. Don't fall asleep, not in here. Sleep is poison. Motherfucker won't ever catch me nodding. He can come for me in the daylight or in the twilight. I don't give a damn 'cause I'm ready. Been ready since sixty-seven."

Brenndan's eyes opened in slow motion. "I'm not sleeping, just resting my eyes."

"Well, rest with them open."

I was beginning to wonder whether I was in a jail or an asylum. All around me, I noticed for the first time, the inmates leaned blurry-eyed against their cells.

"That's the preacher." Brenndan answered my unasked question. "He says we shouldn't sleep because that's when they come."

"When who comes, B?"

"The dreams, man."

Impatient with this junkie's gibberish, I turned to leave. I would come back when Brenndan was sober, but for now I had to leave him, for my own sanity, to the dreary world he was living in. I knew that I had no hope of making a connection with Brenndan in this state. I said good-bye and called the guard to come and let me out.

As I left, a flash of guilt fired in my mind. Isn't that what I had always done? Left my brother to the hell-ish place that he was in, while I moved inconspicu-ously through some other, posher world. And wasn't I just here now because he was going to die, just waiting for the court to set a date and couldn't let him go with all that on my conscience? But I also knew that my brother and I were different people and I couldn't suffer his fate for him. I was as help-less as he was.

As I walked away, the man in the next cell con-tinued to scream in his bout of lunacy. Twice as old as my brother, he leaned against the wall of his cell, clinching his hands in anguish as he shouted, "This happened in fifty-six, off the coast of the is-land."

I averted my eyes and hurried down the corridor. The world had promised him a lot too.

I kept going until I reached the open air of the parking lot, my stomach knotted tightly in a ball. Safely in my car, I sped down the empty side of the highway, past commuters who were creating a backlog on the other side. I could not understand why anyone would choose to live so close to a prison. The suburbs had beckoned them with a plot of land and enough space for the dog to run and open skies on clear nights. The irony was lost on them.

Next to every open space was a closed one. Next to wealth—poverty; next to every brother—his brother. I was heading back to the confined squalor of the city while my brother sat confined in the wide-open wealth memorizing the blocking for his death.

I HAD NEVER intended to wait so long before I went to visit him. I had hoped that somehow he had not done it. I suppose I knew he was guilty the whole time and didn't know what I would say to him, but I never thought that when I did finally go to see him the only thing I would really be able to say would be good-bye: *Yeah, it's been real, my man, you take it easy now and don't worry about that basketball you took from me in sixth grade 'cause I won't be needing it and I guess bygones is just bygones and what kind of flowers should we put on the gravestone?*

The first time I remember my brother dying was when I was seven. Brenndan was nine and there was a group of us jumping from rooftop to rooftop. The point of the game was to see who could reach the last house on the block first, an airborne hurdles. Two stories above the ground, my brother was in the lead. But as he landed on the last building, the rotting roof caved in. Brenndan found himself half-buried in the air. When the rest of us finally made it over to him, all he could say was "Did I win?" That was the way he was.

I was always in awe of him. No matter what I did, he had done it first. His life seemed to be a crystal ball which I could look at to see my own future. I knew which jokes my next teacher would tell over and over, which pants I would wear the next year, and which memories I would make.

No matter how closely I followed after my brother or how furiously I tried to catch up with him, he was always there before me and he had always done it better. Nothing I owned was mine. It was my brother's used-to-be, but even Brenndan's seconds were better than most people's brand new.

Then, sometime around seventh grade, he started to go wrong, horribly wrong. People began to try to pull me away from him. "Brenndan's setting a bad example." That's all they said, as if I was too young to understand.

But I knew what the older boys did in their dark clubhouses, nestled in the corners of abandoned buildings, initiating the pubescent into the adult world of stolen cigarettes and girls who would do anything. Just ask.

While he played in this tainted fairy tale and reaped the warnings of the adults around us, I side-stepped his pitfalls. I was profiting from my broth-ers' mistakes, glowing in his failure, and I was happy.

As we got older though, I began to feel a true sense of our separateness. I could see my brother's mistakes for the problems that they had turned into. Our lives were no longer twin but polar. I was never in danger of going to jail because I had gone joyrid-ing in a stolen car. Parents never forbade me from seeing their daughters, and I never tried to take away the hurt.

Take away the hurt. That's what all the players called it when you mixed heroin and crack. It was a kind of crystallized speedball, combining the highs of cocaine and the lows of heroin with the potency of crack. One hit and the light bends at the corners of your vision. Two hits and your head swoons. Three hits and you get lost in all the glow of forget-fulness. Emotions dull and your heart beats all fucked up like a rainstorm. Tired of old insanities, they created new ones.

Whenever people talked about it they just said,

"Take away the hurt." After that no one bothered with names or words or anything else, because they were painless. No more hurting. They left their bodies and minds and went to wherever else they needed to be.

It was never the same drug twice and you never knew exactly which of its elements would be the strongest. One batch could send you on a three-day trip to the edge of a Martian channel, while a different one and you were deep inside your own womb giving birth to yourself and no use coming out, so why don't I just stay like this for a while? Being born.

Tyrell first told me that Brenndan was hooked.

I was sitting outside of my mother's house, on a rare visit, when Ty called out to me, "Yo, bro, what's up?"

"Not much, Ty."

"Why don't we go grab us a six-pack and kick it like old times?"

"Maybe later, man. I'm chilling with the old girl right now. Just came out here to get some fresh air."

"Come on, man, for old times' sake."

"Sorry, Ty."

Ty grew up down the street from us and I had known him since we were both boys. But even then he was never really a participant in our drama. His role was more akin to spectator than anything else, sharing in our exploits only through a vicarious sense of pleasure, a bulimic who gained satisfaction by watching other people eat.

"Say, Robert, what's the difference between a drunk and an alcoholic?"

"What?" I gritted my teeth in preparation for the same tired punch line.

"A drunk ain't gotta go to no goddamn meetings."

I laughed uncomfortably as Ty slapped me on the

back. "Come on, man. Let a brother hold a dollar. I know you making that long cash."

"Can't do it, Ty."

"All right, man," he said, letting me off the hook. "Say, what's Brenndan up to?"

"I don't know. Haven't seen him for a while."

"He still taking it away?"

"What?" I spun around to face him.

I knew that my brother was not exactly a model citizen, but I never thought he would fall so far down that he would start fucking with that shit.

"No. I don't know." I put my cigarette out and hurried inside.

It's not that I had never suspected Brenndan of using hard drugs, or that he would be incapable of committing the crime that he was accused of. I simply was not prepared when it happened. Instead of making me seek my brother out, Ty's message made me stay even farther away from him. No, not B, that's my brother, only people who have been beat up from the get go, knocked down before they could walk. . . . I knew Brenndan had had problems in the past but that was just mistaking recklessness for courage, alienation for rage, and disaffection for bravery. It was what some boys do to grow up.

Then the call from my mother in the middle of the night. "What? Sure, take all the money you need. I can't be there though. Important deal to close. New account. But Friday, after we sign the contract."

Friday gave way to Saturday and Saturday to Sunday. Then a month of weeks and weekends. Half a year of important deals, until the district attorney was seeking the death penalty. Looking to spill some blood, to send a message, and it wasn't just any blood but my brother is, and the only thing left to say was "Good-bye, Brenndan."

When I finally found the strength that I needed to face him it took almost two weeks of visits before we could say anything meaningful to each other, or manage to re-create any semblance of the bond that we had once shared. It was a different connection though. We were two people who had known each other a long time ago. Now when we regarded each other it was in the way that you eye an ex-lover, or someone else whose body you had forgotten. And when we finally moved through the past, the bits of our lives which we shared were only veins showing through the skin. You still couldn't see the blood beneath.

Maybe the closest we had been since childhood was a visit in prison when Brenndan mentioned his drug use to me. For as long as I had known he was addicted, we never spoke about it. Junkies do not like to talk about junk unless they are talking to other junkies, and then only to find ways to cop or discuss some shit so good everyone is dying from it left and right, but not them because they know how to handle it. So when he finally named his demons out loud, it felt like a special acknowledgment of the shadow bonds that still held us together.

I went to see him on the Monday after the last hearing of his trial. I had not gone to the actual hearing because I could not bear the thought of sitting in the courtroom as one lawyer tried to turn Brenndan into a monster and another turned him into an imbecile. Couldn't look at his face when the jury came back with his life on a piece of paper, smug attempt at stoicism on their faces, my mother crying no matter what they decided, pictures of the boy's dead body passed around one last time, in case you missed the part where the vocal chords pushed through the slit in his throat.

I knew that my brother had sat perfectly still in the stand, nothing on his face but boredom. He would never beg like a dog for his life. He knew that it would only give them the satisfaction of seeing him beg. The jury members in a murder trial were like so many vultures waiting for the first opportunity to rip the corpse apart. I could not watch this scene. It would break my heart.

When I arrived at the prison, the guard ushered me in as usual. The same smell of urine and sweat wafted through the halls. Not the smell of bathrooms and lockers, but a deep-down funk that could only have come from a frame made of steel beams, reinforced with a bum's cold piss collected from a dark alley in the middle of winter, and walls piled from cum dried hard in pure August sunshine, then cut into bricks. I felt reflectively that my brother was doomed.

When I reached his cell, he sat quietly leaning against the back wall reading. I could tell that he had not relented in the vigil against sleep. Eyes closed at the corners, pushing back into the head, rings puffy and etched dark against his skin. This haggard look only reinforced the criminal quality of his prison uniform.

He must have been a nightmare for his attorney. Goddamn Brenndan, can't you act right just once in your life instead of fucking everything up with pride and stupidity and God knows what else you got in that thick-ass skull of yours sticking out like the thorns of a cactus?

As I approached him, my brother did not look up but kept staring at the ceiling of his cell even after the metal bars had clanged open and shut again. I stood there uncomfortably for a full minute before he acknowledged my presence. But when he finally did, I could see that he was struggling to hold everything together.

"They gave me life," he said, cutting through all of the bullshit.

"Motherfuckers gave me life without parole, man."

"That's great, Brenndan. Brenndan, that's wonderful." I reached out to hug him, to pull him near me because I really did care about him, but he did not acknowledge my comment or my gesture. He kept talking as if I were not there at all, only him and his three walls and anyone else who happened to be listening.

"The first time I got high I was kicking it with some niggers from Cabrini. I just wanted to try, to see what all the hype was about. Little Walter put it in a wooden pipe and passed it around; I only got two hits but it was better than anything I had ever done. Better than fucking, man, you hear me?"

"Brenndan," I said, "I don't need to hear about this. I don't want to hear about it. You're not going to die and that's what's important right now."

"The fuck you don't. You been waiting your whole life to hear about this, waiting to see just how fucked up I could get. Well, this is it, man. I smoked the shit, I blew it, I based it, I shot it in veins I didn't know I had. Sometimes I hated myself because I couldn't stop, but you know what? You know what the simple truth was? I loved the shit. It was magic. I would sprinkle it on a bitch's pussy before I ate it, have her so turned out she couldn't talk for a week, and when she finally come around again, the only thing out of her mouth was 'Brenndan, Brenndan.'"

"Brother Brenndan." The voice from the next cell thundered out. "I have seen this before. Seen young men like you beaten down."

"Shut the fuck up," my brother boomed back.

"Ain't nobody beat me down. I wanted to see what it was like, wanted to feel everything, do you hear me? Everything. What you seen, you crazy-ass old man?"

"I have seen the waters of Africa receding as I moved toward a certain death in the water."

"You ain't seen shit except the backside of your black ass."

"No, no, brother Brenndan. You can't lose your faith now. This is the hour when you must either sink or swim. There is no escape. You must hold on.

"I threw myself off the slave ship, only to be reborn; to walk to another death. I was born again in the wicked institution of slavery in the ironic position of being my master's son. I have walked on both banks and everywhere is the same. No escape."

"Listen," Brenndan cried back. "I ain't asked to hear your crazy stories, old man. I ain't trying to hear them either. You ain't nothing but a strung-out junkie. Here." Brenndan tossed a small bag into the man's cell and I could hear him as he scampered for it, not like an animal, but like a man broken by too much city.

I listened as he inhaled greedily, murmuring to himself, "I am *r-r-r-r*," and the thought he was trying to form was aborted by his brain as he exhaled a stream of dead smoke.

"You know why they stay awake?" Brenndan pulled my attention away from the old man. "You know why we stay awake?"

"No, B, I don't." He looked like a child.

"The dreams, Robert. All of us have the same god-damned dream. The people in it is different but it's the same fucking dream come around over and over whenever we try to sleep, and as soon as you wake the first thing you do is try to forget the dream. See, it's a happiness box, man; when you're inside it everything is the way you wanted it to be since you was a little kid. But when you get outside again, as soon as you stop, all the hell that was going on outside comes back on you. It comes back, you can't get away from it, and dreaming it is the worst part. That crazy old nigger got that right, ain't no escape. No running from it and can't live like that." His eyes began to puddle and I wanted to kick him for sinking so far beneath humanity. I hated my brother for his crimes but more than anything I hated him for being in here.

"You know what the worst part of it was?" he asked, straining through a sob.

No, Brenndan, I don't know. I don't want to know. I turned around and walked away.

There was no motive to my brother's crime. The child was still clutching the five-dollar bill that his mother had given him to buy bread with.

Hurry up and run to the store before dinner gets cold. Don't you dare stop to talk to little Missy down the street, and you better bring me back my change this time.

Yes, ma'am.

The boy tried to cut in front of Brenndan in the checkout line. Brenndan cut a two inch deep, three inch long gash in the boy's neck. It was a fairy's wing across.

Maybe the boy's face was set in exactly the right way to stir up for my brother the intense hatred we usually reserve for people whom we have known for years. I could not help wondering if maybe the face he saw was mine or my parents' or simply his own. Something in that face though was stirring up memories that should be left alone.

What anger was carved so deep in him that it consumed everything else? I can't pretend to answer.

My father, in secret, blamed my mother for spoiling him as a child. My mother, out loud, blamed my father. She said it ran in his family, every other generation, just like twins. Both of his younger brothers had gone crazy—Sylvester, who died before I was born, in Vietnam, and Richard in hatred and confusion after he lost his brother. Who knows what Brenndan saw in the eyes of that child or in the dark edges of his dreams? Or what the imagination of the city had thought up to put it there. Had the sight of a banker's suburban driveway spilling too easily into a Chicago street that ended at the feet of a homeless fourteen-year-old mother driven him to the insanity that he needed? Or had he merely done that thing he was born to do? Put on earth to mutilate and destroy, hand just following the command of destiny. There is no map of the human heart.

The area that we grew up in was an almost perfect cross-section. The upper middle class and the working class and all of America's ethnicities shared a neighborhood which was two miles long and three miles wide. It was bounded by the river on one side, a park on another side, a museum on its third side, and a housing project on the fourth. In the center of the neighborhood, and anchoring it, was a well-endowed university. Brenndan and I grew up with an infinite number of paths to choose from. He chose a methodical journey into hell. I stepped over him.

I had smoked dope with him a few times when I was in college. For me it was a joyride, a two-hour escape from logic and a complete adherence to desire, but my brother's need was not to escape logic, it was to defy belief. If there was a risk to be taken he had to take it or spend the next two weeks regretting it. "I want to feel everything," I remember him saying to the old man, and that's how he lived his life.

That is why he had walked through his death so many times. Because in so many years of trying to escape himself he knew that he would someday venture too far. He knew that he would never be truly satisfied until he had walked a gangplank and fallen mercilessly into the waters.

Vacationing in the Caribbean I had watched as so many dark bodies fought their ways through squalid streets, headed toward a grave which promised to be equally dilapidated. I had viewed these scenes with the patronizing romance of one who is safely removed from the fire. I wanted a connection to these people, wanted to share pots of curried goat and warm lager in Trenchtown because I was one of them.

"Black people gonna rise up."

"I and I."

The whole time just an advertising executive on vacation—bring the revolution, and yeah, make sure it wears blue 'cause blue looks so nice on camera. Camera pulls up slow over the water to a shanty bar and ad man drains beer from bottle, mirrors all cracked and no reflection 'cause him all cracked up inside.

The common ancestor had split into a thousand different lineages, each one different. My only bond was a memory, which was quite different in the minds of the other branches than in my own. The plant turned in on itself, determined to defy any attempts at understanding.

My brother turned the carnage inward, hellbent on self-destruction. Secure in his hell, he mocked me. He was a menacing testimony to what should have become of me, what had become of so many.

※

Yet as much as I despised my brother, I needed his approval in the same way that I had once needed the approval of those black bodies in Jamaica. When that approval did not come I was not surprised. From their vantage point I was mocking each of them with my success, which had come on a road they had shunned or that had shunned them. I understood their hatred of me.

Going through an old photo album borrowed from my mother, I found a picture of Brenndan and me in high school. At a time when we had already grown solidly apart, this picture was a rarity not only because the two of us were together but because the photo seemed natural, unposed.

I examined the expanse of his arms around my neck in the picture. They were long and slender, even the elbows were tight with smooth skin, slightly uneven in color, but strong and beautiful. It was the Fourth of July and we had been in mutual rebellion of the occasion. I was fourteen and Brenndan sixteen, a time when no one knows which place you occupy. We were too old to play with the younger kids and too young to be taken seriously by the adults. We were also upset that our parents had insisted that we come fifty miles out of the city with them to my aunt's summerhouse, a place we both despised.

In protest, we spent the day behind the garage, well away from the rest of the company, playing one-on-one basketball. As we left the court we walked affectionately neck in arm. In the picture B looked especially happy. The sun had given his skin a reddish glow and a layer of sweat accentuated the cut of his chin. His head was thrown back in laughter as the two of us shared a moment completely unaware of the camera. We seemed happy, but more than that we looked genuinely close. I took the picture out of its plastic covering to have a copy made.

When I got the picture back a week later, I wrapped it in green tissue paper as a peace offering for Brenndan. Headed for the prison, I took the gift along with a sweet potato pie that my mother had made for him. As I figured out what to say when I arrived, the suburban landscape passed in a blur: concrete highway turning into strip mall, family cars with dogs in the backseats, a family holding a picnic in an open field, completely unaware that the field ringed other lives, the lives they had left the city to get away from.

I still had no idea what I would issue as an apology as I pulled into the prison parking lot. I supposed that the picture would have to be my voice. I hoped that I could communicate to my brother the closeness which I still felt toward him. I wanted him to know that I would stand by my blood. Because that's the way we were raised. And for once I was going to be the person that my parents taught me to be, but this is Brenndan's song.

As I walked down the corridor the inmates leaned blearily against their bars, hoping that the visitor was for them. As far as I could tell, they still had not slept. Even though the body demands sleep in the same way that it needs food or touch, the inmates claimed to fight against it. Maybe they stole catnaps, each out of sight of the others, heeding the law of the body. That's what crimes were, an obedience to desire. For the inmates in cell block 265, this was particularly true. Theirs were the worst of crimes: rapists and murderers, they had no control over their own inner violence. No, they all allowed themselves the sleep, which their bodies craved, then faked a sullen drowsiness for their cohorts. No dream could he bad enough to scare them off. Nothing on the inside so worth avoiding, no lucidity so worth gaining.

I could not imagine my brother, after twenty-seven years of doing exactly what he wanted, suddenly frightened off of sleep by his own dreams.

Looking at the scarred faces of these frightened and sleepless men, I wished for a younger Brenndan, mapping his childhood faces onto the other inmates. I saw my brother at age twelve, now in the shriveled eyes of a man with a pockmarked face and a creeping smile, then quickly blocked the thought. Brenndan had always had a boldness which would prevent him from being pitied.

When we were children, it was Brenndan who sparked my interest in the world, a place which will always be a storybook to him even though he deserved it far more than I. I replaced the criminal's face with the image of Brenndan, at age ten, teaching me the most powerful utterance in the Jamaican ghettos, something that he learned from the reggae records he was immersing himself in at the time, the phrase which got me through my visits there with some semblance of solidarity with the people around me: "I and I."

I forced myself to remember that he was not some stranger but my brother, whose smile warmed me. I nodded limply at the inmate and moved on.

I approached Brenndan's cell as a grisly moan from his neighbor greeted me. "Water, water, water," repeated again and again and again. The guard ignored him and we moved on.

When he finally opened the door of my brother's cell, Brenndan was lying facedown on his cot, confirming my suspicions, showing exactly how much he could resist sleep.

"Browne, you got a visitor, wake up," the guard

said, pushing him onto his side. Brenndan rolled over and I smelled the blood. His tongue drooped from the side of his mouth, dried saliva icing it, holding it like moss. The guard turned him onto his back and I closed my eyes in pain. Can't watch this. Can't see it—not again—imagined it too much, been to close to this for too long, can't watch it. Sheets all soaked with Brenndan's blood, junkie's hypodermic needle sticking in the center of his chest, safely lodged, just below the heart.

The guard rushed down the hall to get help with the body, and I turned to follow him, to get out of this prison. A hand grabbed me and pulled my head into the bars and refused to release it until the whisper of an old man's voice had passed.

My name is River. I have seen this before.

I left my house under a setting half-moon. I knew that when I returned I would be different. I would be hardened by the world.

The town was prosperous. We did not find it strange that these men without color should come here to do trade.

Now they wage the most awful war on us. Our weapons do no good. They know that each man has a certain greed which he will do anything for. They have found this place in each of us. They attack from the inside.

The queen sent her children away in fear. She gave each of them a seed before they left and promised that it would grow.

Wazee, wanasema, wakati unaone kitu kibay kando ya utaona kitu nzuri. Hapa ninaona saamba ni saamba na kitu nzuri ni kukula na kuishi. Mioyo wa watu wauzi ni kali. Siku ingini tutakuwana uhuru wangu.

The old people say that wherever you see something bad, there is always something good next to it. Here, the good thing is to eat and to live. The heart is strong.

※

When we see what blood we spill, we call out to the gods, but they have forsaken us. We shout to the ancestors; only the sound of waters answers back. We are left to the mercy which we have for each other.

We wait. In time, the bodies will rise from the waters.

Eshu has abandoned them. The water does not sound back. They lie in their huts, in mansions, in the street. They run from fear, die from blues. All around, the city that promised hope falls in ruins. They hold on to each other growing stronger, refusing to make peace with any more dead. They plant corn in the garden. They root in the soil and do not move. They grow.

I can see them. They walk through the streets of the cities with a new secret inside. They swagger and sway and cut you dead for looking at them the wrong way. When they return home at night, they rub the bark of the tree which grows in each of their hearts. They planted it; it grew.

I was stillborn. My body passed into the soft mud floor. The barren ground grew pregnant with my seed. I lay down my weapon and ran into the jungle. It is all one life and one memory. The chain of backs spanning it is unbroken. Together, they speak in one human voice.

My name is River. At night I hear their voices, huddled close to each other. The memories beat louder and louder against my skull. Above it all, I hear the wailing, see the water.

Distant from each other we die. I hold my dead close to me like memory but the memory blacks out, more than anything—it refuses to speak. The seed planted in slavery blossoms in the cities. I smell the blood.

I killed my brother. I squandered my love. Nothing I do can hurry me home.

My name is River. This is my blood.

RIVER

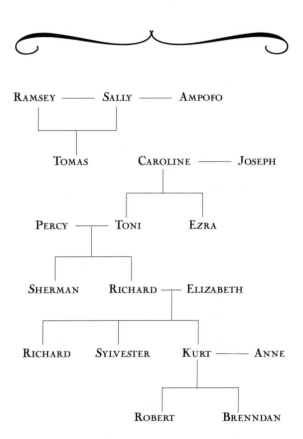